Words Bubble Up Like Soda Pop

Kyohei Ishiguro

YEN ON

New York

Words Bubble Up Like Soda Pop

Kyohei Ishiguro

Translation by Kevin Gifford
Original cover design by Nawada Kouhei

SHOSETSU CIDER NO YONI KOTOBA GA WAKIAGARU
©Kyohei Ishiguro 2020 ©FD/CA
First published in Japan in 2020 by KADOKAWA CORPORATION, Tokyo.
English translation rights arranged with KADOKAWA CORPORATION, Tokyo, through TUTTLE-MORI AGENCY, INC., Tokyo.

Yen On
150 West 30th Street, 19th Floor
New York, NY 10001

Visit us at yenpress.com • facebook.com/yenpress • twitter.com/yenpress
yenpress.tumblr.com • instagram.com/yenpress

First Yen On Edition: July 2023
Edited by Yen On Editorial: Leilah Labossiere
Designed by Yen Press Design: Eddy Mingki, Wendy Chan

Yen On is an imprint of Yen Press, LLC.
The Yen On name and logo are trademarks of Yen Press, LLC.

The publisher is not responsible for websites (or their content) that are not owned by the publisher.

Library of Congress Cataloging-in-Publication Data
Names: Ishiguro, Kyōhei, 1980– author. | Gifford, Kevin, translator.
Title: Words bubble up like soda pop / Kyohei Ishiguro ; translation by Kevin Gifford.
Other titles: Shosetsu cider no yoni kotoba ga wakiagaru. English | Words bubble up like soda pop (Motion picture)
Description: First Yen On edition. | New York : Yen On, 2023.
Identifiers: LCCN 2022056007 | ISBN 9781975352776 (trade paperback)
Subjects: LCGFT: Light novels.
Classification: LCC PZ7.1.I8726 Wo 2023 | DDC [Fic]—dc23
LC record available at https://lccn.loc.gov/2022056007

ISBNs: 978-1-9753-5277-6 (paperback)
978-1-9753-5278-3 (ebook)

10 9 8 7 6 5 4 3 2 1

LSC-C

Printed in the United States of America

Table of Contents

Sakura petals,
they fade on the wind without
a word of farewell

Fireworks shoot up into the sky, colorfully erasing the darkness of the night. The August countryside is bathed in red, blue, and orange. Once every year, during this oppressively hot and humid season, the shining lights turn the gray walls of this huge, inorganic factory into a dazzling array of colors.

A woman in a flower-patterned *yukata*, and a man in a factory work uniform.

They sit next to each other on their picnic blanket, just as colorfully illuminated by the light spreading across the night sky.

Red, blue, orange.

He takes his eyes off the fireworks for a moment to look at her. She responds in kind. The distance between them slowly shrinks. Their lips meet. The next moment, there is a hard, metallic *clack*. She covers her mouth with both hands, cheeks burning bright red. Smiling gently, he shakes his head. The hands at her lips slowly fall away, and then their smiling faces gradually move closer together.

Another hard *clack*.

Their lips never part.

On fated July
of my seventeenth year here,
I ran into you

"The faraway sky, sun flickering high over the green rice paddies."

In a small voice, I try saying the haiku that comes to mind, making a conscious effort at it.

Through the balcony window, I can see blue sky and white, puffy clouds. I can't see the green rice paddies in question, since it's blocked by Building No. 4 across the street, but I think it is a nice touch to represent them on this day, framed by those giant clouds.

Today is July 20, a Saturday, and my last summer vacation of high school is underway.

My room—here in this apartment, complete with a just-sort-of-working air conditioner—is a little muggy from the heat outside. The notes scribbled with haiku ideas that I've posted on the wall, along with the back issues of *Haiku Monthly* that line my bookshelf, look like they're all sagging—struggling in the high temperatures. The only other thing there is a stack of cardboard boxes labeled Arakawa Moving Center, standing out in their spot in front of the window.

My part-time shift begins at one PM today. I need to get out of here soon.

I put on my fanny pack—my current favorite—and grab my phone case off the desk. It's a dual-tone wallet case I found over at Toy Box the other day; I bought it on impulse because the mint-and-vanilla color scheme spoke to me, somehow. The cool thing about this case is that it's designed to hold a small book on the other side; it's perfect for holding a *saijiki*.

There's one other important item on my desk, too: noise-canceling wireless headphones. They never play anything, but I put them around my neck as usual. Giving a nod to my mother as she calls, "See you later!" from the dining room, I leave my sweltering bedroom.

After passing through the apartment complex, I come across the main road that cuts through my local neighborhood—something pretty characteristic to suburbs like this one. Farther along the road, my view opens up to a wide field of rice paddies. I'm on the sidewalk, heat bouncing off the asphalt with no shade to speak of, and I'm walking toward the paddies as usual.

As I follow the ruts in the farm path, I start to hear the familiar sound of the irrigation canal. The paddies are all covered with lush green rice plants, the rustic smell of water and leaves growing thicker. For me, it's an annual reminder that summer has well and truly arrived. Suddenly, I spot something at the base of the plants. Ripples spread all over the water, like it's raining. But it isn't.

"A water strider..."

I take my phone out of my pocket and open up the case. My phone is on the right side; on the left, my saijiki. I had never heard the term *saijiki* until I began writing. Basically, it's a dictionary of seasonal words and their meanings. When you're writing haiku, expressing the season is a must, so every poet from amateur hobbyist to published professional has one of these. There's an app version for smartphones, of course, but I kind of feel like an analog book is easier for me to use. I borrowed this one from my dad, by the way.

So I flip to the index and look up *water strider*.

P. 215 Summer / Animals

Water Strider—water horse, river spider, water spider, purifier
Water strider strong, bobbing in the corner of the raging torrent
—Keiji Hashimoto

...Instantly, an idea strikes.

I promptly open my phone to launch the Curiosity app, quickly tapping away before pressing the POST button. I didn't forget the "#haiku" hashtag, of course.

* * *

Cherry @ Haiku account

Ripples bequeathed by
water striders thrust across
the pallid surface
#haiku

"Cherry" is my nickname. Someone gave it to me because my last name happens to be Sakura, which means cherry blossom, and before I knew it, I was Cherry and that was that. By the time I started carrying a smartphone around in middle school, Curiosity—the short-message social network—was taking the world by storm. My timeline was always filled to the brim with posts sent by other users, and even now that I'm seventeen, the Curiosity boom is still going.

Looking at my timeline, I can't help but think it all over again. Curiosity really *does* suit me. I don't really like conversing and I'm definitely not very good at it, so I feel a lot more comfortable communicating via text alone.

In fact, I had my first encounter with haiku through Curiosity. I happened to see one from a famous poet on my timeline, and it felt so free—a lot more so than my imagination would ever allow. I'd always had an image of haiku as this antiquated culture, and even in my language-arts classes, it never really clicked with me. But when someone commented on Curiosity that haiku is "like capturing a moment in a photograph," I managed to grasp it. For our generation, which is so accustomed to smartphone cameras, that comparison fits really well. And when I tried my hand at a few haiku, I was surprised by how easily it came to me. I've been submitting my work on Curiosity ever since.

My follower count at the moment is…four. The number of likes…negligible. Ah well. I'm doing this for my own satisfaction, so it's all good.

I look up. In front of me, across from the paddies, is a large box-shaped building. This is where all the locals gather, and it's where I'm headed right now—the Oda Nouvelle Mall, a huge shopping complex, part of a national chain you can find anywhere in Japan. I work a part-time job there at

Sunnyside Day Service, and even though I'm on summer vacation, my daily life pretty much takes place inside this huge mall.

Ba-ding. A notification. What is it?

[Curiosity]
Maria ☆ liked your comment.

Right, yeah. There is *one* person who likes all my comments.

It's my mom, but still…

After changing into my work clothes, I walk through the breezy, air-conditioned mall and head for the Central Court on the first floor. Sunnyside Day Service is connected to it.

Sunnyside is an elderly care center; senior citizens who aren't decrepit enough to require an old folks' home come here during the day to eat, relax in a bath, do exercises and training to retain their mobility, and so on. Last month I joined the part-time crew working with the seniors who come here, but really, I'm just supporting the full-timers more than anything.

"Good morning."

Nami, the care manager, turns toward me energetically as I walk into the store, her eyebrows perked up. "I'm in soooo much trouble!" she wails. Same as usual, then.

"Cherryyy," she says, waving her hand. "I know you just got in, but…" She puts her hands together and bows in an apologetic but strangely playful manner, her fluffy blond pigtails swinging. She must be six or seven years older than I am, but she seems so young to me.

"I think Fujiyama's gone on one of his expeditions again. He's probably somewhere in the mall."

I knew it.

"Namiii!"

Akiko, a junior staff member under Nami, comes over from the back of the room. She sports a carefree, short haircut and a ton of ear piercings. The juxtaposition always amazes me. Both she and Nami are former delinquents, I heard, but they aren't the slightest bit scary; they're nothing but kind and friendly to the regulars at Sunnyside and me. Their lighthearted banter is sometimes a bit too much for me, but I appreciate that they give me my space, communication-wise. They never get too deeply involved in my life.

"What's Mr. Fujiyama always looking for?"

"He said something about looking for his record."

"Record? Like, this kind?" Akiko made a big circle with her hands.

"Yeah, probably that. Something like a really big CD."

"Probably?"

"He didn't give me much detail."

"Ah…"

I listen to their conversation in silence. Then, with a quick, "I'll go search for him," I turn and leave Sunnyside.

Mr. Fujiyama is a quiet old man who frequents Sunnyside. He has shaggy hair, like a dandelion's fluff, and reading glasses that always seem to be slipping down his nose. He's also my haiku mentor—not that he's teaching me techniques or anything. We just chat about haiku, is all.

I learned only recently that Mr. Fujiyama's hobby is haiku. I still remember how moved I was when I first saw his work on a wall-hanging scroll at Sunnyside—*New year in morning, life exploding only when golden years arrive.* Exploding? And was the word *only* implying that's what Mr. Fujiyama felt? What *does* aging feel like?

I was filled with questions and curiosity, so I mustered up the courage to talk to him, and that's how things began. Mr. Fujiyama is a man of few words, a lot like me, and we've come to spend a lot of time together.

Recently, Mr. Fujiyama had started wandering—or strolling—around the mall alone, looking for a record.

I go up the escalator, looking down at Central Court as I do, hoping to find Mr. Fujiyama. He isn't around. Instead, I see a group of students my age, along with some children who look like elementary school students. The permanent sofas in the mall corridors, where groups of elderly people and housewives often sit and chat, are currently being occupied by these kids, who are turning it into their personal gaming space.

An arcade, a food court, cafés, movie theaters, clothing stores, homeware stores, free Wi-Fi, air-conditioned comfort, and comfy sofas. No wonder everybody comes here when they're free.

When I reach the food court on the third floor, I find it so crowded that I can't believe it's just after noon. The sound of happy chatter and clinking dishes violently assaults my eardrums.

So noisy...

I look all over the food court, but I can't find Mr. Fujiyama. I found him here last time, but no such luck today. So I go out to the adjacent outdoor terrace, but I don't find Mr. Fujiyama there, either. Instead, there's only a group of lounging old men and some disorderly students.

The terrace is shaded by a roof and lined with metal tables. It has a wide-open feel, and the view is pretty nice. But it's basically outdoors, and the summer heat and humidity sticks to you like duct tape, so there aren't many visitors out here during this season.

I take in the countryside view from the terrace. The farm road that I usually walk down is glistening in the reflected light of the irrigation canal. Nearby, a mass of white dots flies into the sky, undulating and changing shape—a flock of egrets.

I follow them with my gaze, focusing on them as they move farther and farther away from me. The green plains stretch on forever. The ridges of Mt. Oda cut a zigzag line across the horizon. Against the deep blue of the sky, the iridescent clouds resemble a sort of giant flying fortress. Having a high vantage point like this makes the vastness of the area really apparent.

...I'm leaving this area next month. The reason is a pretty common one: My dad got a job transfer. I have no regrets or attachments to this town, so

I don't mind. No real sentimental feelings toward this familiar scenery, stuff I've been looking at since I was a child.

Maybe Mr. Fujiyama left the mall, I think as I look at the rice paddies.

As I search the mall's second floor, I hear a voice calling out, "Cherryyy!" with this weird, cutesy intonation. I turn around and see a life-size cutout of Hikaru Amanogawa, aka Hikarun, a very popular pop star, peeking over the railing of the stairwell. Hikarun's cute pose and smiling face seem to say, "Look at me, look at me!"

"That doesn't sound like her voice at all."

"What? Seriously?"

A boy's head pokes out from behind the sign. He's half Mexican and half Japanese, with almost wheat-colored skin, blue eyes, blond hair like Nami's— he cropped his, but anyway—and a mischievous grin on his face.

"...Beaver..."

I've known Beaver since before I started kindergarten, even though we're a few years apart. He's always restless, and sometimes he gets on my nerves, but I don't hate him. He lives across the street from me, by the way, in Building No. 4.

"That Hikarun cutout is from Toy Box, isn't it?"

"Bingo!"

Toy Box is a trendy shop on the second floor of the mall; I bought my phone case there. It's characterized by its chaotic mishmash of everything from pop-idol goods to books on various subjects for serious fans. The life-size cutout of Hikarun, part of some collaboration between her and Toy Box, was on display at the shop as of a bit ago.

"They'll yell at you again for taking stuff without permission."

"But *Japan* wants it. They just left it in front of the store for a long time, y'know? And he's too much of a wimp to make off with it himself."

He's aware that's stealing, isn't he?

"Beeeaverrr!"

Suddenly, an angry voice rings out. I know this one, too.

"Ah shit, it's Ex-Princess!"

Beaver takes off in the opposite direction of the voice, clutching Hikarun in his arms. The floor manager of the mall, whom everyone calls Ex-Princess, follows in his wake with a face like someone possessed. "He used to work at the Princess Hotel in Naeba," Nami once told me, "so that's why they call him Ex-Princess! How lame is that?" Then she had a little laugh over it.

Ex-Princess, who also has blond hair, is dressed to the nines in a suit, but it's a little funny to see him get angry enough to chase after Beaver. After watching them run off into the distance, I walk down to the first floor where Sunnyside is located to continue looking for Mr. Fujiyama, but he's nowhere to be found.

So I move on toward the mall entrance.

Outside, I find a large parking lot that looks like it can hold five hundred or so cars, but the asphalt and exhaust fumes make it way hotter than the outdoor terrace. I weave my way through the rows of cars looking for Mr. Fujiyama, but he's not around. His cotton-ball hair is pretty noticeable, so it would be easy to spot him.

As I approach the entrance to the parking lot along the main road, I feel a sudden drop in temperature. I glance at my feet and realize I'm in the middle of a large shadow. I look up, and there it is—a vertical billboard about fifteen feet high, creating shade and coolness. In the center of the sign is the logo of Oda Nouvelle Mall, a lofty assertion of its presence.

Then I spot something. Right under the logo, there are words scrawled in spray paint. Each letter is sized differently, and I'm not even sure which way it's supposed to be read, but I still manage it.

All the many things up above to look at bring summer with them, too...

That's my haiku. I'm getting a bad feeling about this.

Walking around the mall looking for Mr. Fujiyama, I encounter surprise after surprise. Looking closely, I can see my haiku scrawled on store walls, steel poles, signboards, and all over the place. I haven't done any of it, of course—it was all Beaver. This kid... He's already scribbled all over his secret hideout, and now he's spreading it around. So embarrassing.

Suddenly, the sweat on my forehead trickles down and into my eyes. I look up at the sky and see the sun shining brightly. It has been so hot recently that the newscasters are making inflated comments like, "the highest temperatures ever seen" and "heat stroke cases reaching a record high," or whatever.

Today's heat may be a bit dangerous. Usually, it's easy to find the guy, but of course he makes it harder for me when it's blazing hot... Better find him fast.

Widening my search, I head for the rice fields along the main road.

Going slowly along the wide sidewalk that runs parallel to the main road, I look around for Mr. Fujiyama. There is practically no one out and about on the sidewalk, and I have far more space than I actually need.

Suddenly, I hear the rustling of wings. It's coming from the rice paddies. Looking over, I see a flock of white egrets flying low in the sky. From the terrace, they were just white dots, but from this distance, I can clearly make out their silhouettes, their wings outstretched.

The flock passes over the farm road. Just below it, I can see a big dandelion head in the middle of the field.

...That's not a scarecrow! It's Mr. Fujiyama! ...He doesn't look like he's in trouble. From this distance, I can see him standing there, calm and composed. Thank goodness I found him.

So I cross the main road at a brisk jog and head for Mr. Fujiyama.

As I run toward him, his figure becomes clearer. He's standing in the middle of the farm road, staring at a square piece of paper about a foot wide—a record jacket—in his hands. What he's looking for is the record, the thing this jacket's supposed to hold.

As Nami told Akiko earlier, nobody has a clue what kind of record it is, what kind of songs are on it, or even if there's any music on it at all. I once caught Mr. Fujiyama mumbling, "I want to listen to it again," while staring at the jacket. I guess it must be important if he's looking that hard for it. Maybe it's something really rare.

I rush over to Mr. Fujiyama, who's a bit shorter than me. Leaning down a little to put my face close to his ear, I shout, "Mr. Fujiyama!" No response. He stares at the photo printed on the jacket—a row of cherry trees and what looks like a metal tower—without indicating whether he sees me standing in front of him. I'm used to that by now, but still...

Mr. Fujiyama is extremely hard of hearing. He doesn't bother with hearing aids, though, so it's not uncommon for him to act like this when I talk to him. I don't want to think it's because I speak too softly.

Though actually, I noticed when I put my face close to Mr. Fujiyama's that he isn't sweating at all. There isn't a drop of it on his wrinkled face, and the collar of his shirt looks dry, even in a scorcher like today.

I move closer to Mr. Fujiyama's ear and call out at my maximum volume. He slowly raises his head and looks at me, finally noticing I'm there.

"Did you find your record—?"

"Ohhhh! Cherry, my boy!!"

I immediately cover my ears with my headphones. Mr. Fujiyama really shouldn't shout so loud without warning like that. Keeping them on in anticipation of future outbursts, I try again, "Did you find it?"

Mr. Fujiyama shakes his head. No dice today, either.

"All right. How about we head back now?"

I hold out my hand to Mr. Fujiyama, and he takes it. We walk side by side as we head back to the mall.

🎧

On the way to Sunnyside with Mr. Fujiyama, I notice a crowd of people in the indoor space reserved for events and entertainment. "What's that?" I say, looking at Mr. Fujiyama, but he doesn't seem to be very interested.

This amusement space is on the first floor of a huge cylindrical atrium, with lots of tall vertical space. It's a decent-size venue, and there's always something going on there during the weekends. I think there was a car show not too long ago.

There's a stage facing a pair of escalators that intersect in an X shape, and a crowd of people gathered around it. Almost all the people on the escalators are looking down at the event. A sign over the heads of the crowd reads, in fancy letters, DIAPER SCRAMBLE—BABY CRAWLING RACE!

"Okay! Are all you good little kids ready? Ahhh, but you babies might not understand what I'm saying yet…" A cheerful female voice comes out of the speakers, revving up the crowd. I can hear the voice even through my head-phones; it must be pretty loud.

Mr. Fujiyama and I are watching from a ways behind the crowd. There are so many people in the audience—maybe fifty or so—that we can just barely see the stage through the gaps.

Four or five babies are sitting in a row on the left side of the stage. One of them is restlessly looking around; another is about to start crying at any moment. The men looking on in confusion behind the babies are probably their fathers; they must not be used to this sort of thing. An equal number of women are on the other side, kneeling on the floor, leaning forward as they wave and talk to their babies.

At center stage is a woman who looks like a presenter, clutching her microphone tightly. The voice I heard earlier must have been hers. Hold-ing up the microphone ostentatiously, she says, *"Okay, let's get this started!"* Her voice seems to get the mothers and fathers more fired up than the babies.

"On your mark… Get set… Whoa, hold up!"

Through a gap in the crowd, I can see the babies on the left side crawling past.

"You all have to start at the same time, don't you?"

Of course, the babies don't stop. The whole space fills with laughter.

"Whoa there, babies! That's a false start!"

They're really not gonna understand, lady. You said it yourself just now.

"False start…"

I start whispering to myself. *False start?* What's the term in more native Japanese? *Flying start*…like flying in the air? *Running on ahead. Buzzing too early.* Needs two syllables.

"False start…"

I keep mumbling to myself, beating out the rhythm with my right hand. Is this anything? Can I use it?

I take out my phone case and open my saijiki. Thumbing over to the main index, I look at the entries I find under *F*—which includes *P* and *B* variations.

Buyo (gnat)	Summer 217
***Fuyou (hibiscus)**	Autumn 340
Fuyou (hibiscus tree)	Autumn 340
Fuyoukaru (withering hibiscus)	Winter 452
***Fuyounomi (hibiscus seeds)**	Autumn 346
***Furaki (August 8 – the death of**	
Fura Maeda, haiku poet)	Autumn 321
Furakoko (swings)	Spring 321
Puratanasu (Platanus)	Spring 95
***Burakkubasu (black bass)**	Summer 211
Buranko (swings)	Spring 50
Furando (swings)	Spring 50

Guess *false start* doesn't count as a haiku-centric seasonal word. Surprising that swings are supposed to evoke the spring though.

"…you! …way!"

Suddenly, my ears pick up something. Is that…Beaver I'm hearing through my headphones, through the cheers? It's coming at me so fast that I take my eyes off the saijiki and look over to see…Hikarun?!

Without warning, something hits me. I feel my body go flying as Hikarun brutally pushes me away, crashing into me at great speed.

"Agh!"

Almost at the same time, a girl yells right next to my ear. Who was that? This is a little too much to process…

Boom!

Another jolt hits me, but I quickly realize that it's me falling shoulder-first to the floor. Ouch… I think I might have hit my knee, too.

As I slowly get up, a dull pain slowly spreads throughout my body. I lift my head and look around. From the floor, the mall I know so well looks like an unfamiliar place.

Then I see someone a little farther away from me, in the same pain as I am as she sits up. A girl about the same age as me, with long hair. Was that "Agh!" this girl's voice? ...Ahhh, she's looking at me.

She seems to be kind of dazed as well, unable to figure out what just happened. My head is getting clearer, and I'm guessing that Hikarun—probably Beaver—had run into me at high speed and knocked me over, pinballing me right against this girl, and then she and I both fell to the floor. Come to think of it, this girl's face is so pale it's basically white... Oh, she's wearing a mask, that's why. During the summer, even. You can use masks as a seasonal term for winter, right?

...Oh.

Now I start to see more of her face. The strap around one ear had come off and the other one is clinging on for dear life. The mask dangles a bit before stopping. There's more visible skin on her face now, but still some pure white where her mouth is... Her teeth? With something like a metallic gleam, too. I know what that is.

"Braces..."

I realize I have unintentionally mumbled that out loud. The girl suddenly covers her mouth with her hands and slumps down. Her cheeks turn bright red; her shoulders tremble a little. Then she gets up and hurries away.

I thought she had gone, but then she comes running back, bends down a few feet away from me, and grabs something rectangular from the floor. A phone; the one she'd dropped when I bumped into her. Then she walks away, shouldering her way past parents, children, building columns, everything.

"You okay, Cherry?"

I suddenly snap back to reality when Beaver calls to me. I can hear the cheers from the baby race again. It was so weirdly quiet for a moment there.

I look up to see Beaver standing there with the Hikarun cutout and his skateboard under his arms. "I told you to move out of the way," he says, not looking at all regretful.

"Some more warning would have been nice," I grumble.

"And why the hell do you have your headphones on like that? It's so stupid."

I didn't realize it until he told me, but my headphones had rotated 90 degrees across my head and an earpad is resting on my forehead, probably from the impact of the collision. "Doing it mohawk style, huh?" he says with a chuckle.

"Beaver!"

Multiple screams drown out the cheers of the baby race. I look over to see Ex-Princess and some security guards closing in on us.

"Oh no! Ex-Princess!" Beaver's voice trails off. In no time, Beaver is on the move, speeding through the mall on his skateboard. Ex-Princess and his team chase after him, shouting the whole way.

Before I know it, my pain is gone. As I slowly stand, I look at the spot where the girl had grabbed her phone. Another rectangular object had fallen there, mint and vanilla in color. Even from a distance, I can recognize it. It's my phone.

As I go to pick it up, I see something white right next to the mint and vanilla. Ah, a mask.

I pick up my phone and put it in my pocket, staring at the mask left on the floor. She was so panicked, she probably didn't even notice that her mask had fallen off.

Her braces were so shiny. *Braces. Brac-es.* Two syllables. I reach into my pocket for my phone, only to stop myself. There's no way *braces* is a seasonal word, right?

🎧

As the automatic door slides open, I hear lively voices coming from inside Sunnyside. It's the sound of elderly people enjoying conversation.

Sunnyside is housed in a rented space about the size of a small convenience store. The first thing you see when you walk through the entrance is the living space at the far end of the facility. There are two sets of tables for four people, and in one corner of the wall is a TV and a collection of magazines. There, a group of chatty folks are engaged in conversation. Mr. Sasaki, the most talkative of the men in the group, is looking stylish again today in his cowboy hat. Mr. Genda, a sly grin on his face, always wears sunglasses; I once heard him say that his cataracts make his eyes too light-sensitive. Ms. Miyahara, with her large earrings and fluffy perm, has a gentle, feminine laugh and often likes to give me candy for some reason.

A partitioned space near the entrance has some assistive devices set up. Nami and Akiko are in the process of helping some clients with them. Nami is assisting Mr. Hyoudou, who has trouble walking, with some ambulatory rehab; he's using a set of parallel bars to toddle his way along. Nearby, along the wall, there's a low platform with a handrail; Akiko is there spotting Mr. Souma, who has been suffering from knee problems recently, as he climbs up and down the step.

"We're back."

"Oh, thanks, Cherry. And welcome back, Fujiyama!"

Nami talks to everyone as if they were friends her age.

"Thanks for handling that all the time, Sakura."

Ms. Tanaka, the head of the center, approaches me from her seat across from the assistive-care space, where the office computer is located. She has a calm demeanor, kind of serving as a mother figure to everyone. She's also the one who arranges my part-time shifts.

"Not a problem," I reply.

"Did you find the record, Fujiyama?" Nami asks as she leans against the parallel bars. Mr. Fujiyama turns to Nami and puts his hand over the mouth of the record jacket he held so carefully. He opens it, but there's no record inside. He shakes his head slowly.

"Aww," Nami says, sounding regretful.

Mr. Fujiyama starts walking toward the three-seater sofa by the common space where he usually sits. I follow him.

"Cherry?"

When I turn around, I see Nami pointing her index fingers at her ears.

"Not while on duty, okay?"

…Oh! I hurriedly remove my headphones. I had just been cautioned about that, too. It's hard to converse with the seniors like that.

Catching up with Mr. Fujiyama, I help him sit down on the sofa. This kind of basic assistance is also part of my job. There's no one else on the sofa, and Mr. Fujiyama is small enough that there is a lot of space on either side of him. Mr. Hashiguchi and Mr. Yamamoto are happily chatting at a nearby table, but Mr. Fujiyama is sitting still, uninterested in joining them.

"Guess he didn't find it again, huh?" I hear Ms. Tanaka's voice from a distance. Turning around, I see her talking to Nami on her way to the assistive-care space. "I'm sure he forgot where he put it..."

Ms. Tanaka's expression darkens a little with Nami's next question.

"What should we do about Fujiyama's care plan, chief?"

"Let's discuss it with his family."

"Right, yeah..."

Nami is blunt, as usual, but her expression is serious. I'm not sure what a "care plan" is, but I think I know where this is going. The two of them must be concerned about Mr. Fujiyama's wanderings—his little strolls.

"Emotions welling! As the young man rises up! Above the oceans!"

I cover my ears with my headphones at the sudden shout. Nami had just warned me about this, but Mr. Fujiyama can surprise you like that out of nowhere sometimes. He's just so loud...

"Emotions welling, as the young man rises up, above the oceans..."

Now Mr. Fujiyama murmurs it softly, as if he'd read my mind. I know this. It's a haiku.

"Um..."

Who wrote this one again...? Oh, I know!

"Settsu! Yukihiko Settsu."

"Mmm, hmm-hmmmm."

"Settsu's haiku always have this strange sense of movement, don't they?"

"Putting sound to scenery... What does it mean?"

"Sound...to scenery?" Huh? What's he going on about? This is too advanced for me to understand.

"Um, Mr. Fujiyama, if you could lower your voice a bit from now on..."

"Whaaaa?!"

"...Your voice!"

"My *what*?!"

"...Never mind."

I enjoy discussing haiku with Mr. Fujiyama, but when we get into high-level topics like this, it goes over my head. I have a lot to learn about haiku.

* * *

After that, I stay with Mr. Fujiyama for a while and chat about haiku with him, although it feels more like a Zen lecture than a discussion. It is pretty deflating.

"Hey, Cherry! You here?!"

I hear a gruff, angry voice echoing through the space. It's coming from the entrance. I look over and see a guy wearing a baggy T-shirt, a backward baseball cap, and thick cargo shorts exposing his gangly legs and bowlegged stride.

Akiko smiles and waves.

"Ah, here comes Toughboy!"

"A-Akiko…"

The guy called "Toughboy" immediately drops his attitude.

"Um… Hey. Heh-heh!"

He scratches his reddening cheeks, suddenly acting shy. I don't know how old he is, but he looks about twenty.

"Mr. Fujiyama," calls out Ms. Tanaka, "your grandson is here to pick you up." I help Mr. Fujiyama get up from the sofa and escort him over to Toughboy.

"Akiko…um, hee-hee, like, a *date?*"

Toughboy continues to mumble before noticing I am there.

"Ah! Dammit, Cherry!"

He calls me Cherry, too, even though we aren't friends.

Akiko said that he suddenly started reporting to Sunnyside more often after she started working there. I remember Nami grinning and telling me, "Akiko said to me, you know, 'Nami, isn't Toughboy the lamest nickname ever?' He has no idea she said that, either." By the way, this nickname comes from the words *TOUGH ☆ BOY* written on this T-shirt he wore once. He has it on again today, the words dancing in front of my eyes right now.

"You know where that Beaver guy is, don't you?"

"No."

"That asshole graffitied my car, man."

He pulls his phone out of his pocket and holds it out to me. I wince as it almost hits me in the face. On the phone is a photo of a white car, the words *Toughboy was hear!!* scrawled on it. Pretty big, too.

"Toughboy was *hear*…?"

I think he meant *here*, but whatever.

"Don't screw with me, Cherry Boy! 'Cause I'll rip you apart if you do!"

Toughboy turns his anger on me. Guess he didn't like me reading that out loud. He comes even closer to my face, threatening me.

"…I'm not."

Toughboy looks unconvinced.

"Well, if I see him again, I'm gonna beat his ass! Tell him that for me, man!"

Then he leaves with Mr. Fujiyama. He must have inherited the volume of his voice from his grandfather.

"Well," Ms. Tanaka says, "it's not quite five o'clock, but you can go ahead and clock out now, Sakura."

Oh. Guess I spent quite a bit of time looking for Mr. Fujiyama.

"Okay."

Ms. Tanaka points to her ears with both index fingers and smiles at me, looking distressed… Oh. I rush to take off my headphones.

I change out of my work clothes and leave through the employee entrance. The entire loading dock in front of me is shadowed by the buildings around it; even the large trucks parked there are completely shaded. It is still light out, but I can tell evening is approaching. The heat has eased up considerably.

I feel a little thirsty. I haven't had anything to drink since noon because I spent so much time looking for Mr. Fujiyama. I decide to buy a soda from a vending machine near the entrance. Unsweetened seltzer is all the rage right now, but I'm not a fan. I want just a little bit of sweetness. Unsweetened feels a little too grown-up.

So I buy my usual soda from the machine and take a sip. The moderate sweetness quenches my thirst. It's the best out there, really.

Suddenly, I notice a fence near the vending machine that looks like a construction barricade. It's a steel plate striped with orange and black diagonal lines, and on top of it there's a piece of white cloth with a now-familiar scrawl.

In ultramarine, the blue-and-white flycatcher evokes a straight line.

I posted that on Curiosity last week… Beaver again? He's probably at his secret hideout on the rooftop again today. I had planned to go home, but keeping what Toughboy said in mind, I might as well pay the hideout a visit.

A parking lot on the roof of a shopping mall is a common sight in Japan, but the scenery is so monotonous up there that I almost get lost whenever I come up. The location of the escalators and elevators in the building don't seem to match up in my mind with the accesses to the parking lot. When my father and I take the car to go shopping here, we normally use this lot, and then it takes forever tracking down our car when we're done.

I exit the elevator hall on the rooftop to the lot. There's no ceiling, so the evening sun is illuminating everything. The area in front of the elevator hall is shaded, which helps a little.

Turning around, I look up at the wall of the elevator hall, which looks like a square shed, and see a horizontal blue sign that reads ENTRANCE C. This is the landmark I have to look out for. I glance around. After confirming that no one is watching me, I move to the side. Quickly climbing over a chest-high fence, I take the ramp heading away from the wall. As I ascend, I check again to make sure there are no witnesses. From here, I have a good view of the entire parking lot. A lot of cars are parked there, but luckily there's nobody around.

Climbing up the ramp puts me on the roof of the elevator hall. It's a flat area, about half the size of the sunlit parking lot, and there's graffiti all over the floor. It's all Beaver's scrawls…and it's all my haiku. In fact, aren't there more than the last time I was here?

Beaver calls this place his secret hideout. He keeps decorating it with stuff from the mall stores, and now it looks like someone overturned a toy chest. I don't know how he got it all up here, but there is a child-size shopping cart (complete with a doll of Odamaru, mascot of the city of Oda), a beach umbrella, and even a tent to provide shade. Beaver's always had a habit of bringing stuff here from all sorts of places; that's why I gave him the nickname Beaver. I think his real name is Pablo or Paulo or something, but Beaver fits him better in many ways.

One day, he brought me here, saying, "I found this awesome secret hide-out." There was nothing here at the time, but now there's even a running fan, connected to a reel-type extension cord. It blows air toward the tent.

I can hear Hikarun's voice—the way Beaver imitates it—saying, "Ohhh, Japaaan…" Inside the tent, Beaver is holding a masklike object in front of his face and wriggling his body around. Across from him is a pudgy guy with his arms crossed, staring at Beaver with a pout on his face. He has a head of naturally curly hair, large glasses, and wears an apron from the store Hand Off on the mall's third floor. This is Japan, and he looks a lot like a giant Buddha statue.

I thought Beaver was holding a mask in front of his face, but it is actually Hikarun…or, to be exact, the head of the Toy Box cutout. It's the same Hikarun that'd bowled me over earlier.

"Ohhh, Japaaan, it's me, Hikarun. We're finally together!"

Japan's arms, which hadn't moved even slightly until now, are slowly unfolding. His right hand quickly reaches out to Hikarun, snatching her away.

"Ah! …Heh-heh."

Beaver scratches his head and laughs awkwardly.

"…You're just awful," Japan finally says. His voice is lower than usual, so I can tell he's livid. When I take a closer look at Hikarun's head, which he had taken from Beaver, I notice it looks like it's been roughly torn off. I wonder what happened to the rest of her body, but I soon find it. It is propped up against the tent in a cute pose—headless.

"The deal's off," Japan says quietly (although his anger is palpable) as he gently places Hikarun's head on the floor. Then he picks up a large glass bottle from nearby and hides it behind his back. Inside it is a large amount of Pero-Pero, individually wrapped hard candy that comes in a variety of flavors—Beaver's favorite.

"Hey! Why're you saying that?!"

"Because you tore her damn head off, you idiot!"

"I have the body, too!"

"That's not the *point*!"

Japan's plaintive cries make even Beaver wince. Holding Hikarun's head in his hands, he staggers out of the tent. He stops in front of the horrifying headless standee and tries placing the head back on, adjusting it in ways only he understands. I know he's torn up about this, but...really?

As his Hand Off apron suggests, Japan works part-time at the mall. We didn't know each other at first, but we became friends through Beaver. He says he's nineteen, which makes him two years older than me. Hand Off is a used-goods store that sells electronics, games, clothes, musical instruments, and a lot of other junk that you wonder if anyone has a use for. They have a pretty big space on the third floor, and they keep it decently busy up there. "Sometimes we get guys selling rare pop-idol stuff," Japan had once said, "and I'm not supposed to do it, but sometimes I keep it for myself. Like, I pay the store price for it and all, but... But the other day someone brought in a limited-edition Hikarun keychain that was only available at one of her concerts, so..." Once he starts talking, he just can't stop. He seems to like pop idols a lot. I don't know the origin of the nickname "Japan," but he used to play baseball in high school, so I think it's modeled after Samurai Japan—the name of Japan's national baseball team.

Watching their exchange, I bend down to enter the tent and sit down in the space vacated by Japan.

"Oh, Cherry..."

Beaver helps himself to the bottle of candy while Japan is gone, sampling the wares a little.

"Did you bring that cutout to give to Japan?" I ask.

"Yeah, to trade for this," Beaver says, his mouth watering as he pulls a piece of candy out.

"But you didn't trade anything."

"No, like, I know the head's off, but all the parts are there, so..."

He takes a bite, savoring the sweetness.

"You know," I say, taking a piece for myself, "Toughboy was looking for you a few minutes ago."

"'Toughboy was here!'" Beaver reaches into his pocket and pulls out a black stick that looks like a baton from a relay race. "I wrote it on his car," he says, brandishing the thickest magic marker I have ever seen. Probably oil based. No wonder Toughboy was pissed.

"It wasn't 'here,'" I say before popping the candy in my mouth. "You wrote *h-e-a-r* on it. Toughboy was *hear*, not *here*."

"No, I got it right," whines Beaver. He sure didn't.

The sun is gradually setting, turning the whole area orange.

I move out of the tent and under the umbrella so I can relax on the beach chair. From here, the rice paddies are out of sight, but there's a panoramic view of the large number of cars and the ridgelines of the Oda Mountains. I like the wide-open feel this landscape gives me. Beaver, meanwhile, is scrawling my haiku on the floor with his extra-large magic marker. We follow each other on Curiosity, and he keeps on making whatever I post into graffiti.

"Hee-hee-hee! I'm getting pretty good at it."

"No you're not. Nobody can read that children's doodling," Japan says derisively.

Japan, observing Beaver's scrawls from nearby, doesn't hesitate to make fun of him.

"It's not doodling, dumbass. It's tagging," Beaver retorts.

"What the hell is tagging?"

"Don't you know anything about hip-hop? It's tagging. Graffiti. You know, the fancy text and pictures spray-painted on the walls around here? That kinda thing."

He's right. I do see a lot of spray-painted designs all over town, on utility poles and roadside billboards. But Beaver's graffiti isn't anything like that. It's just really bad handwriting.

"I don't care about hip-hop," grumbles Japan.

"Well, I don't care about pop idols."

"Also, like, isn't this all Cherry's haiku?"

"I'm learning Japanese with Cherry's rhymes," Beaver says, plopping down on the beach chair across from me with a thud as he reclines all the way back like he's in bed.

"You already speak it fine," Japan says quizzically.

"I can't *write* it, man. Dad can only write in Spanish, too."

Beaver is in sixth grade now, so being illiterate in Japanese is probably a big problem. I wonder if they teach him any of that in school.

"Hmm..."

Japan seems convinced.

"You're tagging up the whole mall with my haiku, aren't you?" I accuse.

"Yeah, and all over the apartment complex, too!"

"Stop it, man. It's embarrassing," I complain.

I pick up the soda on the table and take a sip.

"Why not? Your rhymes are really cool."

"They're not rhymes. They're haiku."

I have no idea why he calls them rhymes.

"Yeah, but..."

Suddenly, it becomes much brighter. I reflexively use the plastic bottle in my hand to block the light. The beach umbrella had been shading me earlier, but now the sun is low enough in the sky that it is shining right in my eyes.

I can see the evening sun through the clear soda bottle. Bubbles, and the setting sun. Almost dreamlike. Sunset... No.

"...Dusk."

Dusk might be a better way to express time and space in one go. Now I need some color description...

"The dusk..."

I try saying it out loud. I'll definitely fit it in somewhere.

"Got a new one brewing?" Beaver says, latching right on to me, but I don't feel like dealing with him right now. I just let it go as I take out my phone. Curiosity has a draft function. Let's write this bit down for now.

I open the case, and as usual, I go to launch Curiosity...

"Huh?! Whose phone is *this*?!"

I notice right away. This phone has a familiar-looking case...but it's definitely not mine! The two-tone mint and vanilla colors are the same, but the phone itself is a different color from mine. There's no thickness to the case, nowhere to put an entire saijiki—just a couple of cards. How did this happen? I've been carrying this thing all afternoon...

Suddenly, I flash back to the collision at the amusement court. Skin revealed under the white, that glint to her mouth...

"Braces..."

"Now what...?"

I stare at that girl's smartphone case, at a total loss. Not only did I lose my phone—it's guaranteed that someone else is gonna look at it, too. So hard to deal with... But then, she can't unlock it, can she? But it'll have that saijiki inside... Maybe she'll think it's weird. It's like someone is peeping into my bedroom. I hate it.

I go back inside the tent, trying to hide all this. Beaver and Japan must have noticed something is off, though, because they both come into the tent and sit down on either side of me. It's cramped enough as it is, but with all three of us sitting in it at once, the sardine-can feeling is off the charts.

Her case is the same brand and color scheme, but this one has a mint background with a star in a similar color. I recognize it. It's a limited-edition piece that came out early in the spring, a little more expensive than their regular lineup, but I think it sold out pretty quickly.

"What's up?" Beaver asks.

"I think I picked up someone else's phone."

I suppose *she* did first, to be exact, but...

"Someone else's?"

"Yeah...I think when you bumped into us."

"Oh, it's my fault?"

Beaver is as unapologetic as always.

Riiiiiing...

Unexpectedly, a call comes in.

"It's ringing," Japan says calmly.

"Huh? What do I do? What should I do?!"

"Why don't you just answer it?"

You make it sound so easy!

"I...can't," I say, my voice cracking. I'm completely losing my mind!

"You don't have to unlock it to take a call, y'know."

Japan has a lot of techy knowledge like this.

The phone screen displays the word *Julie* and a cutesy icon of a face wearing glasses. Is she a friend of that girl's? I mean, I can pick it up, but I'd just be talking to Julie. It wouldn't get me any closer to this phone's owner…

Ah!

"Hey!"

Beaver forcibly takes my phone. Then without hesitation, he presses the ANSWER button on the phone screen and returns it to me.

"Here you go."

"Hello?"

And he went out of his way to put it on speaker mode, too! The girl's voice echoes across the tent. Huh? Actually, this voice reminds me of the *"agh"* I heard from that girl.

"Hellooo?"

"Ah…uh…" I'm still too nervous to speak!

"Um, can you hear me?"

"Mm…?"

Japan brings his face closer—or, really, just starts staring at the screen. "She asked if you can hear her?" Then his index finger goes straight for the phone and presses a button on the display.

"Whoa! What're you doing?!"

The voice on the other end of the call sounds extremely panicked.

"Marie! Where's my mask?!"

She sounds really agitated about something. But Marie? Not Julie? The button Japan pressed didn't change much on our end. The icon of the glasses character just went full screen, is all.

"Huh? What? What's going on?"

Japan doesn't respond to me. He's been staring at the screen for a while. "What's up?" Beaver asks, moving his face closer to look at the screen.

Suddenly, the icon goes away, revealing a group of three girls.

"Ah…"

The one in the middle is the girl I know. Oh? She's got a mask on.

"Um…"

"Um!"

We speak up at the same time, our conversation faltering from the start.

"So I think you have my phone…"

The mask hides her mouth, but it's crystal clear that she's distressed about this.

"Smile for me!" Japan yells suddenly in a pretty off-putting way.

"Oh, she hung up."

Just as Beaver had said, the screen switched to an end-of-call screen just after Japan's outburst. "Awwwww," he pouted.

"What the hell? That sure was gross of you."

Beaver shoots Japan a scornful look. But Japan, sitting up, doesn't even look at him. "For real…?! Like, seriously, that was Smile, wasn't it?! And Julie and Marie, too…! Is Orange Sunshine back in business?!"

He's mumbling to himself, perhaps unable to contain his excitement, as his body trembles.

"What are you rambling about? Hey! Japan! What's this 'Smile' and 'Orange Sunshine' stuff about?"

"She's a teen influencer on Curiosity! You know her, Cherry, don't you?"

I shake my head. I don't know anything about this. What is it?

"You're really that stupid?! Her streams are super popular on Curiolive! They're these three super-cute sisters, and they used to do kid-oriented stuff like toy unboxing videos, but lately Julie and Marie—oh, Julie's the oldest sister and Marie's the youngest. Smile's the middle child. So then, uh, where as I… Oh! Right! Lately, Julie and Marie haven't been streaming at all; it's only been Smile in front of the camera, so there're all these rumors about internal strife and so on. But I never believed any of it, y'know? Orange Sunshine is a really tight-knit group!"

I don't understand half of what he's saying.

"Smile's been streaming solo for a while now, but she's still really popular! I think she's broken a million hits overall—"

Riiiiiing…

"Pick it up, pick it up!"

Japan points at the phone, clearly excited.

"No, I can't…!"

While I'm fumbling around, Beaver once again hits the ANSWER button on his own.

"What the hell, man?!"

"Agh!"

Oh, crap! I shouted too loud.

"No, um… That wasn't meant for you, um…!"

Beaver must have hit the video call button because unlike before, Smile and the others are already on the screen staring at me…looking offended.

"No, uh… I'm sorry…"

I always yell and scream at the exact moments where I shouldn't. I'd never make this mistake on Curiosity, at least. It's all text.

Such are my thoughts as they glare at me reproachfully.

Summer's lustrous sheen, there's a false start in the wind and the evening dusk

"Can you hear me, everyone?"

I press the START button and kick things off with my usual question for the listeners. When I talk with a mask on, it rubs against my cheeks and chin, which is a little uncomfortable. Also, if I leave it on for too long, it starts to hurt my ears—but when I started using ones with cloth straps instead of rubber, it got a lot better.

I hold my phone up high to make my face look smaller, so the image on my phone is mostly floor, with me wearing a mask and looking up. The screen's shaky because I'm walking while streaming this, but this is a brand-new phone my dad just bought me, and it has some kind of stabilizer thing which helps eliminate screen shake.

At the bottom of the screen, listener comments are scrolling from the bottom to the top. The number of comments is…well, actually pretty impressive. I've only just started, but it's over a hundred.

I can hear you perfectly!

Wooooo!

Of course!

Your voice is so cute. Smile! ☆

A parade of comments pours in, one after the other. I've been using Curiolive since I was little, so I'm pretty good at following the comments with my eyes.

You have a mask on again, huh?

Do you have a cold? I'm worried.

Maybe one of those pollen things?

Everyone's concerned about the mask today, too, I see... I know they're just worried about me, but it's still kind of annoying. I'm not gonna tell the listeners, but I'm not wearing this mask because I have a cold or hay fever. It's to hide these not-so-cute braces.

Around half an hour ago, I was at the Tama Dental Clinic on the second floor of the mall, opening and closing my mouth as instructed by the dentist.

"All right, now I'd like you to say 'eeeeee,' please."

"Eeeeee..."

The light shining from above blinded me.

"Open wide... *Aahhhh*... Close... *Eeeeee*..."

Can this just end already?

"Okay, you can relax now."

The moment he said it, I stretched my upper lip down as far as I could to cover my front teeth. The area under my nose felt so stretched out that I must have looked funny.

"Do you feel uncomfortable at all?"

"...Nhooo."

Hiding my front teeth as I talked made me sound weird.

"All right, that's all for today. I know brushing is going to be a little tough for you, but don't forget that you can gargle with mouthwash when you need to, all right?"

"...Awrr raiii."

I couldn't even say "all right" correctly.

"Okay, see you at the next checkup."

Once payment was dealt with, I didn't bother waiting for the receptionist to finish saying, "Have a good day," before fleeing from the office.

The Tama Dental Clinic is in kind of a secluded area, deeper inside the building instead of along the main section. This area houses the Nouvelle Hall event space, a travel agency—stuff like that—and not many people frequent it. Right next to Nouvelle Hall is a dead end, just some benches along the wall, and that was even more deserted. I quickly ran for it, checking the area again to make sure no one saw me, like I did when I came here.

…Okay, all clear.

I took out a rectangular packet from my favorite day bag (the grape-green color is so cute). SUPER COMFORT! WON'T HURT YOUR EARS! it read. Just as I was about to unseal it, I heard a tinkling sound. My hand stopped for a moment, but I regained my composure and pulled the white mask out from the packet. From this point on, my mask handling was superfast. I opened the mask, put it over my ears, and secured it over my mouth. I'd been doing this every day for about six months now, so I was used to it.

There's nothing left in the mask packet anymore. This was the last one. I'll have to stop by the pharmacy on the way home and get some more.

I took my phone out of the pocket of my shorts (it's a pain to fish for it in my bag). I bought a new case to go with my new phone, a two-tone mint-and-vanilla notebook case. It's actually a limited-edition design. Normally, the mint part is just a plain mint color, but the one I bought has a slightly darker ☆ printed on it, and it's really cute! Just a casual little ☆, nothing flashy or ostentatious—it looks stylish. It's also kind of a nod to my last name, Hoshino, which literally means "star field."

I opened the case and launched the camera, going into selfie mode so I could see myself on the screen. I checked to see if the mask was on properly. No problems there. It wasn't exactly flattering, but at least it hid what I needed hidden.

"Okay," I said out loud, brightening my mood. I felt like my normal self now, except for the mask.

"Can you hear me, everyone?"

I come out into the mall corridor along the stairwell, launch the Curiolive app, and start broadcasting. The number of comments, which was around a hundred earlier, has increased to around two hundred. I have around three hundred likes as well. Curiolive is designed so that when a viewer presses the

LIKE button, a funky little ♡ floats up from the bottom of the screen, and I see a lot of ♡s flying around me right now. Right. Let's get started.

"All right! Are you smiling every day? I'm Smile from Orange Sunshine— Smile For Me! ...Wow! So many likes! We're already over a thousand! We're going wild today, huh, guys? Thank you *so* much for all the likes. I can't even see myself anymore because of all the hearts. Hey, I can't read the comments when they go that fast! Calm down, everyone! But thanks again! Today's visitor count is...6,589 people! Oh, 6,710... It's going up too much to really know. Anyway, I'm going to introduce you to some of the cute stuff I found today, okay? If you think something's *really cute*, please like or comment on it. So yeah, I'm at the local mall today. I just switched cameras, but can you guys see this okay? This is, um, let's see...the second floor! Right where the atrium is. Oh, the corridor? The second floor is where all the clothing stores are. There might be more people than usual since summer vacation starts today. I'll have to be careful not to bump into anyone. Um, the camera... Can you see me now, guys? All right, let's all go in on this... Smile all the way!"

Curiolive is so much fun! Everyone knows all about me. Isn't that just totally amazing? All these people from across Japan—maybe even the world— on the other side of my phone, and I'm hanging with all of them right now. All the viewers are joining in with comments like "smile for me" and "smile all the way." Like, it's just text, but it really *feels* like I can hear them, sorta. You'd never see this kind of thing in real life.

I want to share all the "cute" that I find with everyone. And with Curiolive, it's just so easy! And fun!

"Oh, look at this! A tiny vending machine. Cute!"

There's a vending machine along the third-floor walkway, maybe meant for kids? I have to kind of half kneel to get to its height. I guess malls have lots of families visit them, after all.

"Here's a Hikarun cutout. Isn't Hikarun super cute?"

I like Toy Box a lot. I bought my phone case there, in fact.

Then when I come to Southern Court on the first floor, I see this huge collection of *daruma* figures! There's this open plaza next to the escalator where they sell local specialties from all over the world, but today they are selling daruma. It's a local specialty here in Oda. My hometown! Odamaru looks like a daruma if you squint hard enough, doesn't he?

There are all kinds of daruma on display, from big ones to small ones, even pink and white daruma!

"Daruma... So cute!"

...Huh?

Cute...?

Cute! (ha-ha)

Pretty funky...

It falls into the cute category?

Hey! Commenters!

"No, really, these daruma are super cute!"

I'm not sure if my sense of cute is off or not. But I'm sticking to my guns! Daruma figures are cute!

Speaking of which, there's one display that I'm curious about. It looks like some kind of big machine, really. It's so large that I can't even reach from one end to the other with my arms outstretched, and the whole thing is made of some kind of steel plating painted green. There are things like drills and discs attached to it, and if you go around to the back, you find buttons and monitors over there. Plus, this kiosk (which I really can't call a kiosk) is covered in daruma.

"What is this thing?" I ask the viewers.

?

Some kind of machine?

Looks like a robot!

And so on. But well, it sure isn't cute, so whatever. So in search of more cute, I take the nearby escalator back to the second floor.

"This is the information sign. Looks like an app icon, doesn't it?"

There is an information booth in the middle of the mall, the sign displaying a stylized, cute "!" so you can easily spot it. I like it a lot.

"Look at that! A cart train!"

There's a row of colorful children's carts with Odamaru dolls on them at the cart drop-off next to Kato Books. It's like an amusement park or something. Odamaru's kind of got a "so ugly it's cute" design, but the little carts absolutely kill me! Now I kind of want to ride in one.

Suddenly, I hear a lot of what sounds like laughter and cheers from the atrium. That's the amusement space, isn't it? It's on the first floor, just opposite the Central Court. I didn't notice the noise until now.

So I run to the stairwell and head for the area. The cheers are getting louder and louder. Putting my hands on the lattice fence attached to the round stairwell, I look down at the first floor. Wow! A huge crowd! There must be an event going on.

There, I see babies crawling, lying down, crying, and laughing in the middle of the hall. The crowd around me seems to be gleefully screaming at the sight of them.

"A crawling race! That's so cute!"

I decide to check it out.

When I get off the escalator and arrive...

"Wow! So many people!"

It's surprising. Seems like more people than I had seen from above. Not that I'm short, but I can't see any of the babies from here...but this is when a smartphone comes in handy. I switch from selfie mode to the normal camera and hold it up with my arm outstretched. That way, I can see over the audience...but it doesn't really work. I try adjusting my angle but to no avail. Just too many people!

"Beaaaverrr!"

Suddenly, a shout cuts through the cheers. I reflexively pull my phone down. Who is it? Who's calling me Beaver? I heard it from above me, but I still can't see who's yelling at me.

"Whoa!"

The voice comes from just to the left of me, and the next moment, my phone and I are knocked into the air. I fall to the floor hard, feeling pretty helpless. So many things happen at the same time, so I'm very lost... It's a hard floor, too, so it is quite a shock. Pain spreads to my shoulders and lower back.

As I slowly get up, I look around. I see lots of legs and feet; they belong to the spectators at the crawling race. That, and a boy's eyes. He's about the same age as me, rubbing his shoulder and saying "Owww..." as if he, too, is picking himself up after a fall. We are the only ones at the same eye level, here by the floor.

One thing that bothers me a little is that this guy has some headphones on, but the way he is wearing them is really odd. The part that goes over his ears is on his forehead, like he's sporting a mohawk.

"Braces..."

I didn't miss it. His voice was so tiny, but I would *never* miss it.

My place is less than a ten-minute walk from the mall. There's a large rice field in front of the mall, but the land actually all belongs to us. My family's been farming here for quite a long time, and now my father and uncle are the ones running it. The farm road functions as a shortcut to our house, and I always use it to hit the mall.

The ruts in the farm road slowly come to an end. I'm walking with my head down, so I'm not looking ahead, but it's not dangerous because no one comes along this path but me anyway.

At a small bridge over the canal, I stop. That guy's voice echoes in my mind. My face gets hot again.

"...He literally said, 'Braces,' out loud!"

I am so embarrassed that he saw my teeth that I all but scream. Wait. My mouth feels oddly exposed... Ahhh!

"My mask! Where is it?!"

I hadn't even noticed, but at some point my mask had come off and disappeared somewhere. When I bumped into him, I guess? I'd know if I gave it some thought, but I was so flustered back there that I didn't know what to do. Good thing there's nobody around the rice paddies. I'm about to take a mask out of my bag when I remember, oh, right, that had been the last one.

…I *knew* my teeth would stand out. He said *braces* and all, but if it were just my buckteeth, I bet he wouldn't have said anything.

I take my phone out of my pocket. I don't even need to put it in selfie mode to see them. My face is reflected in the glass of the screen. Those big, beaver-like front teeth, and the braces. I don't want to see it, but I can't help but check on them… Wait.

"Huh? Whose is this?!"

This isn't my phone! Mine has slots on the left side of the case where I keep my train pass, but the one in my hand now has a book in it that I've never seen before.

A memory flashes back to me. That guy with the headphone mohawk.

"Headphones…"

This must be his phone. I made a mistake…

I close the case. Just as I thought, there's no ☆ in the mint backdrop. I open it back up. I'm not sure what this *Seasons* book is, but it looks like a dictionary or something, maybe? It's full of words that I don't recognize, all with these cryptic descriptions… Oh, wait!

"My phone! I must have left it there!"

I hurry back to the event space, covering my mouth with my hands. The baby race is over, and the place is deserted. I look for the place where I had picked up my phone earlier, but nothing is there—not just my phone, but my mask is missing, too. I ask the information desk on the second floor if they have received any lost items. They haven't seen my phone.

What should I do…? Not having my phone is *bad* news. My heart is in chaos. I feel nervous. My eyes settle on the "!" atop the information center.

…Then it dawns on me. That's right! Marie can help!

I head home at once to ask my sister for assistance.

"Hello!"

When I get home, my mom and dad say, "Welcome back," at the same time. I run through the living room and up the stairs, shoot down the second-floor hallway, and go right into our room.

"Marie! Help me!"

When I enter the room, my gaze meets not with Marie but with my older sister, Julie.

"Quiet, Yuki. I have a practice exam tomorrow."

Julie is studying in the common area in the middle of the room. She's a high school student, one year older than me, who'll be taking college exams this year. I figured she'd apply to art schools because she likes art, but as she put it, "I try to keep things balanced, you know? I just want to keep that stuff as my hobby."

Julie's kind of a fashionista; she knows a lot about clothing brands and stuff. Her hair's a little curly like Dad's, but I think it's cute, and her big glasses suit her face well. Our room has no partitions, and it's pretty large, maybe 350 square feet. My dad asked the architectural firm to design it this way so the kids could get along better. My space is on the right side, Julie's on the left, and in the middle is a large round table and three chairs. We all study here, and even when we're not, we often gather here to chat. Marie hangs out here a lot, too…but today she's nowhere to be seen!

"Where's Marie?!"

"Huh? Isn't she in the loft?"

I run up the stairs leading to the loft. That's where Marie's space is, and mine is just below it.

"Ah…Marie?"

She isn't there, either. Where did she go?!

"Yes?"

I hear Marie's voice coming from the play space (as Mom calls it) across from her area.

"What's wrong, Yuki?" she asks, licking away at a lollipop.

"Marieeeeee!"

I run into the play space connected to the loft, hoping to ask Marie for help ASAP. I nearly collide with her. "Hey! Watch out!" She's a little taken aback.

"Marie, please! Find out where my phone is!"

I pull the phone out of my pocket and show it to Marie.

Marie gives me a strange look.

"It's right there."

No it's not!

"It's not mine!"

I tell her everything that's happened.

"Oh, man, losing your phone sucks. I would die."

She turns toward the computer in her space, ready to begin searching for my phone. She likes playing online games on this PC, which is a hand-me-down from Dad. She's only in eighth grade, but she's learned a lot about the internet from Dad, so she's pretty good at that stuff. "We can just follow its GPS signal to find it," she tells me, but I really don't know what she's talking about.

Marie wears her long hair in two buns on the sides of her head, and whenever she moves her body, they sway to and fro a little. It's a really cute look.

"Not having a phone wouldn't actually *kill* you, you know..." Julie, who was studying downstairs, is now playing with her phone as she sits on Marie's bed.

"*You're* not the one who lost it! I'm totally gonna die!"

Does Julie not understand how I feel? Also, like, doesn't she have a practice exam tomorrow?

"I'd die, too." Marie nods as she sits at her computer, her buns bobbing a bit.

"If I don't get it back by the end of the day, I'll die!"

"Found it!"

"Really?"

Her monitor has a map on it, prominently featuring a smartphone icon with the words *Yuki's phone* under it.

"Is this—?" Marie brings her face closer to the screen. "—the mall?"

"The mall!"

I'd just looked over there, too!

"You find it?" Julie joins us at the computer.

"She said it's in the mall! I'll head back over there!"

I'm already running as I say it.

"See you," Marie says cheerfully.

"Why don't you try calling it?"

Julie's suggestion makes me turn back and reply, "I *told* you, it's in the mall!" She looks down at me from the loft, pulls out her phone, and beckons me to join her.

"If you call it, maybe someone will pick up."

Oh, I see. If I use her phone to call mine, whoever found it might answer! *You're so smart, Julie! No wonder you're applying to universities!*

"Well, I'm glad you got your phone back."

"Oh, man, so am I. I had no idea what I was gonna do…"

"Good thing you didn't die, huh?"

"Yeah!"

It's Wednesday, July 24, and Julie just told us, "I can't possibly study any longer today," so me, her, and Marie are hanging out at Niagara Café at the mall for the first time in a while. The waffles in here are so good—I love it when they pair it with mint chocolate ice cream. It might be summer, but I take my herbal tea hot. I feel like that goes better with the waffles. Marie asked for a waffle with berry sauce on it, and Julie goes for a plain waffle with a vanilla topping.

Like Julie just said, my phone is safe and sound. After that video call, we met up at the amusement space to trade phones. It was weird, though. That guy… Like, he didn't say a word the entire time.

"Yuki, what's with the way you're eating…?"

"New trend or something?"

I have to take off my mask to eat the waffle, but I don't want people to see my teeth, so I am covering my mouth with one hand while I eat.

"It's fine, okay?"

If I don't want people to see me, *I don't want people to see me*, all right?

After we enjoy our waffles (as hard as it was for me to eat), we leave Niagara Café and wander around the mall with no particular destination in mind.

As we do, Julie asks, "Do you really hate people looking at you that much?"

"Yes. It's too gross."

"Your braces make you look like a cyborg, Yuki. It works for you. You'll be a lot more popular."

Great. Marie's acting like my live stream producer again. "Noooooo," I whine, interrupting her.

"You know, those buckteeth were one of your charming points back when you were young."

"Yeah, but…"

"Yeah! The viewers loved it. That beaver smile."

"I'm not a beaver."

Beaver Smile. I liked that nickname back when I was little. I thought it was cute.

I started streaming on Curiolive six years ago, when I was still in elementary school. I knew Curiosity had a video streaming service, but it was Marie who first got me interested. "I heard that Curious Kids (the kid-oriented streaming service on Curiolive) is really popular in the US!" she said. None of us had smartphones back then, so Marie had no choice but to beg our dad for one. Dad was into the idea, too; he always enjoyed that kind of thing. Mom didn't look too happy about it, but Marie pushed so hard that she finally said yes, too.

She started out by introducing some of the toys she'd bought with the money she got from relatives for New Year's, and when Julie and I saw her and Dad streaming and carrying on in the loft's play space, we asked to join in. We called ourselves the Orange Sunshine sisters, and once a week, we'd do a live video—basically just nothing but unboxing and reviewing toys, so the play space got full of them pretty quick.

Marie was popular for her hair buns; Julie for her curly hair and big glasses (that hasn't changed at all!); I, on the other hand, was known for my big front teeth, which I got from Dad. When I smiled, lots of people commented that my front teeth stood out like a beaver's, which made me look cute. I don't remember who came up with "Beaver Smile" first, but eventually the "Beaver" part got edited out and "Smile" became my handle.

Julie made up the little "Smile For Me" pose that I do. I think she said she borrowed it from a girl band that was popular at the time.

Streaming as a trio was a lot of fun for me…but Marie got bored of it pretty fast. So she quit Curiolive, saying it was more fun for her to stream gameplay videos instead. Julie, meanwhile—the best student among us—began calling it a waste of time. So in the end, I was the only one left, and now I've been streaming solo for about two years.

Me talking by myself wasn't enough to get people motivated to watch, so I decided to use my streams to introduce the cute stuff in my life. Once I got started with that, it was surprising how well it was received.

Most recently, I began to start really hating my front teeth—the teeth people called "cute" and "like a beaver." It all started with a comment from Dad.

"Y'know, Yuki, if you hold your mouth open all the time like that, people are gonna yell at you to stop spacing out, like they do to me."

I *thought* I was keeping my mouth closed. But ever since Dad brought it up, I suddenly got super self-conscious about my front teeth—like, if you think about it, they really *are* the most ridiculous buckteeth ever. What's worse, if you look at my face from the side, it's *so* obvious that they're sticking out at an angle. Totally non-cute.

Once I noticed that, there was just no turning back the clock. I couldn't stand how awful it looked…so I asked Mom and Dad, and they agreed to let me get braces.

Unlike a retainer, I wouldn't be able to take these off until the treatment was done. They'd be clacking away, all messy and gross, the entire time…and having people see that is so embarrassing. So I resolved to cover my mouth with a mask—and ever since then, I can no longer take it off in front of anyone but my family.

"But I thought you liked your front teeth," Julie says.

"I *used to*…but, like, they're not cute at all."

I'm sitting on an open three-seat sofa by the escalator; we are all taking a break.

"Puberty hit you like a ton of bricks, huh?"

"But you don't like your braces, either?" Marie asked.

"No."

Of course not. They're *gross*.

"But they're cute. Very mecha."

"Marie!"

Don't call them mecha!

"Well, I kinda get it. Sometimes, you wake up one day and suddenly you hate how you look."

"Did that happen to you, too, Julie?"

"Yeah. And I'm sure you'll get it, too, Marie. Like, 'Ohhh I hate being so small…'"

"Awww, I hope not."

The conversation between them goes on and on, but I'm in no mood to join in. I gaze off into space. There are a lot of people around today.

"…Ah."

Across from the sofa, there is a group of old men and women passing by a clothing store. At the very back of the group is that boy with the headphones. He is wearing the same clothes he was wearing the last time I'd seen him.

"Hey, that guy…!"

"That's the guy we met!"

Julie and Marie notice, too. For some reason, they begin to sneak behind me, as if trying to hide.

The guy stops with his head down and stares at something in his hand. He looks conflicted, somehow… Oh, he's looking at his phone screen. The group of old people moves on, not noticing he's stopped.

"Hmm?"

Julie and Marie both say it out loud at the same time. A woman with long, beautiful black hair approaches the guy and stops. He notices her, too, saying something to her.

"Hmmm?"

Julie and Marie lean out from behind my back, pushing me forward a little.

"He likes older women, huh?"

They seem oddly disappointed about that. Certainly, she seems older than him, maybe thirty years old.

"So he has all those problems with talking, but he still has a girlfriend?"

Huh? That's his girlfriend?

"Maybe it's his sister?"

"Nah, they don't even look alike."

They are busy swapping theories behind me, but I recall when he got a look at my front teeth. "*Braces*." He'd said it in the tiniest whisper, but I'm sure that's what he said.

Suddenly, I feel something around my mask. I realize it is my finger, held over my mouth and the mask. I look up, and I see he has just walked away with the long-haired woman.

So I get up from the sofa and follow them.

The guy, the long-haired woman, and the group of old people are gathered on a wide bridge-type thing that connects both sides of the main mall corridor. The group and the guy are sitting on a long sofa, while the long-haired woman stands across from them, talking about something. The three of us are hiding behind the stairwell railing, watching them. It is just glass between us and them, so we aren't exactly inconspicuous...but they don't notice.

"All right," the long-haired woman says, "now let's share what you've come up with in the midst of that excursion."

Excursion? What's that mean?

"Please write your work on the strips of paper I just gave you. I'll read them for everyone this time."

"Miyuki," the guy in the cowboy hat says, "is it all right if we don't write our names?"

So the lady's name is Miyuki. I wonder what kind of teacher she is?

"I'd prefer if you did, if possible. We'll put these up on display over at Sunnyside later."

Sunnyside?

The people sitting on the bench start to write something on their papers. The headphones guy is joining them.

"All right, I'll collect them as you finish up."

Miyuki walks toward the bench and collects the paper strips—the young guy's last. He is looking down at the floor like he doesn't want to be there much.

"Great! Now I'd like to read them for you."

Returning to where she was, Miyuki looks back at everyone else. I can only see her back from where I am, but with a flick of her hand, she holds the strips of paper to her chest.

"*The mall mannequin, wearing a yukata at the bright shopping mall. The mall mannequin, wearing a yukata at the bright shopping mall...*"

Is this...poetry—haiku or something?

"Is she a language teacher?" Marie whispers. "We're not at school," counters Julie.

"So the mannequins at the store window are dressed in yukata, or light kimono, and it feels a lot like summer, doesn't it? I can certainly feel that. This is by Mr. Sasaki."

The old man in the cowboy hat scratches his cheek in embarrassment, the people around him smiling and applauding.

"Moving on..."

Miyuki stops for a moment. She is staring at her stack of papers, shuffling from one to the other. After a while, she looks at the headphones guy and says, "Cherry?" He responds with a look of surprise. Cherry, huh? Is that his nickname?

"Could you come join me here a minute?"

"...Okay," Cherry replies softly, standing up and starting to walk over to Miyuki. Once he arrives, she offers him a strip of paper. Cherry takes it, mumbling, "This...is mine...?" to himself. Why is he so puzzled about it?

"If you could read it for us, please?"

"Huh?!"

"...You don't want to?"

"No, I mean... I'm just not into reading in front of people and stuff... Like, it's not really my style..."

Cherry is clearly upset by Miyuki's request.

"But everyone wants to hear it."

Miyuki turns toward the bench. The old people there all nod and smile. That elicits a very obvious change in Cherry's facial expression. His skin turns bright red—right, like a cherry. He looks more agitated than before, slumping down, sighing heavily, staring at the paper in his hand, and acting all restless. It isn't just his face that turns red, but his entire body. His arms, visible below the sleeves of the pink polo shirt he is wearing, are the exact same shade.

"Why don't you read it to them? You have such a wonderful voice."

Once Miyuki says that, Cherry turns toward the crowd and holds the strip in front of them, resolved to his fate. It is hard to see his expression, but I can tell his ears are the color of red bricks. Oh, man. Just watching him makes me nervous.

So there he is, holding up this piece of paper as his shoulders tremble, but he is having trouble getting started.

"...The..."

Huh? The? He said something, but I couldn't hear it properly.

"...The...away...rays of..."

"Ehh?"

The old folks cup their hands around their ears.

"A little louder, Cherry," asks Miyuki. Cherry stands up as straight as he can, takes a deep breath, and exhales loudly. Then he holds up the strip of paper again, his shoulders shaking even more than before. Even from this far, I can tell how hard he's straining.

After a few moments of silence:

"The shopping mall melts away amid the crimson rays of the sunset!"

He plows through it pretty quickly. The group members look at one another, then smile and clap for Cherry. His shoulders are still shaking, but his skin has managed to return to normal. And maybe it is just my imagination, but it's like I can feel waves of anger shooting out from his back.

"Thank you very much," Miyuki says softly. I glance at her face; it kind of feels like she is saying, "Sorry to force you into that," with her eyes. Without making eye contact with her, Cherry returns the strip of paper and walks back toward his original seat. Then he stops midway.

"...Haiku," he says assertively. Everyone, myself included, listens. "...Haiku's an art that uses the written word... They don't have to be read aloud..."

With that, Cherry puts his headphones over his ears. It's pretty awkward.

"...True," Miyuki says softly, "but don't you think there are some aspects that can only be conveyed when you say them out loud?"

That startles me a bit. Things you can only convey when you say them out loud... I don't hear the comments from my viewers. I just read them, and I assume that lets me understand their feelings. But what if I misread them?

Cherry's mouth moves slightly. It sounds like he is saying something, but I can't hear it from this far away.

"Voice of the cicada! Even reaching the ears of the girl in the mask!"

The dandelion-headed old man near Cherry suddenly shouts so loudly that the people around him visibly flinch... Wait. Is he looking at me?

"Voice of the cicada, even reaching the ears of the girl in the mask..."

Now he is slowly pointing at me. Cherry and the rest of the crowd look in our direction. Oh, crap! They caught me peeping on them! And not just me, but Julie and Marie, too. My sisters freak out, standing up and sitting down as they try to hide behind the glass (not that they could!). Then they finally give up, and we all say, "Sorry," in unison.

That evening, for some reason, Cherry and I decide to walk home together. "We'll go home first," Julie and Marie say, giving me sinister smiles.

Normally, I'd be nervous about going home alone with a boy. This farm road I usually take is like my own little world to me. I can tell I'm acting strangely self-conscious around him. I thought it'd be a little awkward to walk too close to him, so I step along the far right edge of the path and Cherry takes the left side, across some low grass.

Still, I can see that Cherry is even more nervous than I am. If anything,

I feel like I'm being completely brushed off. Like, I've spoken to him a few times along the way, but the conversation's been extremely one-sided so far. Besides…I have something to ask him: Do my front teeth stick out too much or not…?

"So you're one year older than me, Sakura?"

"…Looks like it."

Cherry's real name is Sakura. Yui Sakura. Yui's a pretty rare name for a boy. Yui Sakura. Yui. Sakura… Oh.

"That's why they call you Cherry?"

"Huh?"

"Sakura. Your last name."

"Oh, um…yeah."

And here I thought it was because his face turned cherry red all the time… Actually, maybe that's the origin after all. But after the time we spent at the mall, I feel like that isn't something I should ask him about.

"*Cherry* sounds pretty cute."

Kind of a cute reverberance to it. *Cherry*, huh…?

"*Cherry*… You don't mind being called that, right?"

He doesn't reply, that same vaguely peeved look still on his face. And he has kept those headphones on the entire time. Does he not want to talk to me?

"What are you listening to?"

"Huh?! N-nothing…" He takes them off his ears. "I'm not actually listening to anything."

He's not?

"I've always had a hard time with loud noises…so this is kind of, like, noise canceling for me…"

Aha.

"Plus…this way, people don't talk to me, so…"

So he really *doesn't* want to talk to me?

"Oh, but not that I don't want you talking to me, Smile…!"

Cherry apologizes to me, trying to backtrack; he must have picked up on my feelings.

"So nobody talks to you, huh…? Yeah, that's a pretty smart idea!"

I really mean it, but it seems to confuse Cherry even more. But I kind of get it—the idea of wearing headphones so nobody talks to you. If I have a mask on, nobody's going to talk about my buckteeth. Usually, they'll just think I have a cold or something.

"Summer cold?"

"Huh?!"

It feels like he was reading my mind for a moment.

"No, this is just…!"

I deny it in a panic—but ohhh, maybe he thought that was weird! …Sure wish I could change the subject.

"But hey, why do you have a dictionary with your smartphone?"

…Oh, am I coming on as too friendly now?

Cherry takes out his phone. "Oh, the saijiki?" His case is the same brand as mine, and the same mint and vanilla, but there is no ☆ on it. No wonder we mixed them up.

Still, though…

"What's a saijiki?"

"It's like a dictionary for haiku."

Oh, he smiled a little?

"There's an app for it, too…but I kinda like the book version better."

Cherry opens the case and runs a hand over the saijiki, gazing at it fondly. A dictionary for haiku? I didn't know that existed.

…Huh? Cherry seems to be enjoying himself a lot more now that we are talking about haiku. I feel like an invisible barrier between us has vanished.

"You like haiku?"

"…I post them on Curiosity and stuff."

"Oh, I *so* get that!"

"…?"

"Like, that way, more people will get to see them, right?"

Connecting with tens of thousands of people in real life at the same time is a world that I, a normal high school girl, could never have imagined. But my phone makes it totally possible. I think that's really amazing.

"I *so* understand that!"

Wanting to upload that stuff to Curiosity… That's *so* me.

"I have no idea who reads them…"

Despite my excitement, Cherry is almost whispering, his gloomy face staring at his phone. The invisible barrier has flipped right back up.

"Does haiku come to you quickly?" I ask through the barrier.

"When I'm on a roll, yes…"

"Wow."

Oh, good. He isn't offended after all. I guess it must have relieved me a bit, so I casually ask: "Can you make one now?"

Cherry looks shook. I think that might've been a bad idea.

"Oh! Sorry. That was out of line, maybe."

Cherry has stopped, so I'm a little bit farther down the path, which means I have to look back at him. We are just at the small bridge over an irrigation canal. Sometimes I get asked to do the "Smile For Me" pose while I'm streaming, and it always throws me for a loop. I do it right at the *start* of my stream, after all, not throughout the stream. When people don't pick up on that, it gets kind of awkward for me. Cherry looks really annoyed, too; I think I might have actually offended him this time.

He is looking down a little, with a thoughtful expression. He seems angry, but really, he appears to be off in his own little world. His furrowed eyebrows suddenly relax into a gentle curve. Instantly, I feel like the barrier disappears again. Cherry slowly raises his head and looks at me, but…like, it feels like he is seeing right through me, looking at something farther away…

After a while of this, his head falls again, and he slowly closes his eyes.

"Summer's lustrous sheen… There's a false start in the wind…and the evening dusk…"

A small whisper. But I hear it clearly. The five-seven-five rhythm. Even I can pick up on it.

This is a haiku. One Cherry just made up. It's amazing. He really *can* come up with one just like that. I'm kind of impressed. But there's one thing I don't understand.

"What does 'lustrous sheen' mean?"

It didn't sound familiar to me. Some kinda haiku thing?

"Oh, it's just a way to describe light. It's a seasonal phrase that evokes summer."

Cherry points behind me toward the main road beyond the rice paddies. I turn around to look, and there I see that there are streetlamps lined up at equal intervals. It is evening now, but it isn't that dark yet. The streetlights are on even though the sky is still decently bright, as if signaling that night is about to fall. I usually don't pay attention to this kind of thing, but looking at it this way, it's almost otherworldly.

I try to say Cherry's haiku out loud.

"Summer's lustrous sheen, there's a false start in the wind and the evening dusk…"

…It's funny. I have an image of haiku as being old-fashioned, but this one feels different…

"…Cute."

As I gaze at the lights, I can't help but express my honest feelings.

"I think your poem's really cute, Cherry."

I turn to find Cherry red as a cherry, just like I saw him at the mall. He is giving me this strange stare—and this time, I can tell his eyes are on me. Then his bright red gradually changes back to its original color. He slowly approaches me, still staring. He takes off the headphones.

"…How?"

His voice is dead-serious. So I think about it more carefully. My instincts tell me it is cute, but what is it about this haiku that made me think that?

"The 'false start in the wind' part, for example."

I think there's something cute about that. That's why I said it, but Cherry doesn't seem to get it. His strange gaze doesn't let up.

"In the wind," he mumbles, as if thinking hard about what it means. Oh. I get it. Hearing this, it makes perfect sense to me. Now I know what I find cute about it.

"…Your voice."

"…?"

It may not be haiku-style cuteness, and it may not be a proper answer at all, but I'm certain of it as I tell Cherry. When it comes to cute, I'm always confident in my tastes.

"Your voice! I think it's cute!"

Sunflowers asking what "cute" means, looking it up in dictionaries

What the hell does *cute* mean?

That night I lie in bed, thinking about the meaning behind Smile's words. *Cute. Cute.* That means it's good…right?

"The 'false start in the wind' part…?"

How is that *cute*? The sound of it? The kind of senses someone must have to think that haiku is *cute* amazes me. I sure don't have them. Sometimes I think I come up with cool, sophisticated stuff, but *cute* isn't at all in my wheelhouse…

I stare at the ceiling. This apartment complex is being renovated, and the ceiling is covered with a white fireproof fabric that sags down a little. I extend my right index finger toward the blank ceiling, tracing out *false start* in the air with it. It makes a lot of rounded curves, like in cursive writing; a soft image. *False start* might seem cute to me after all, but Smile wasn't looking at the words. She was hearing me recite the haiku.

Your voice.

"Your voice! I think it's cute!"

I was shocked. I have never thought of my voice as cute. Not even once.

A cute voice… That's more like what Smile has, isn't it? Smile's voice is clear, transparent, never even muffled by the mask she wears. It is a bit high, and sometimes she rambles on a bit, but each word reaches my ears clearly.

"*Summer's lustrous sheen,*" I mutter to myself in my room. "*There's a false start in the wind…and the evening dusk…*"

You can't really be sure if your voice is cute or not when you hear it yourself.

If she's that popular a streamer, I bet Smile's really good at talking in front of people. The exact opposite of me. *She'd* never have a problem reading haiku to an audience.

…Today's haiku meeting was the absolute worst. The haiku I made during our excursion wasn't all that good, but Miyuki still asked me to read it aloud. That was so unreasonable of her.

When I get really nervous, my skin turns bright red. It's always been like that. I first noticed it back in third grade, when I saw a picture of myself at a school choir competition. I got picked to be the conductor for my class's group, and I was so conscious of my classmates and the audience watching me… It was the most nervous I'd ever been in my life. I had buried most of my memories about how I'd looked at the competition, but I think photos have the power to show you who you really are, the bits you can't see for yourself otherwise. My face, as shot from the side of the stage, was so red that I can only compare it to a boiled lobster. My moves and conducting were so awkward, so amateurish, that I looked like a puppet on strings. Neither my friends nor the teacher said anything about it, but I'm sure they didn't want to upset me.

Looking back, I think it was around this time that I began to dislike conversation. Maybe my desire not to embarrass myself in front of people unconsciously led me to shun communication. I don't *want* to be like this. If I could overcome it, I would. That's why I agreed to Miyuki's unreasonable request…

…But in front of everyone, my whole body blazed hot. I could feel all this crazy tension in my shoulders. The strip of paper I was staring at quivered a bit, the hand holding it was wine-red. I felt people's eyes on me, and when I looked up, I locked gazes with Mr. Fujiyama. His expression was the same as always, but his eyes were all like, "I *dare* you to read it."

I could easily replay the words I had written in my head, but when I tried to say them out loud, I felt like a lid had closed over my throat, preventing me from speaking properly. Uttering my words in a patchwork, cut-off fashion wouldn't really get them across to anyone…but when I made my best effort to speak, I wound up going too fast, and I got the idea nobody really comprehended it. All the smiles and applause afterward just made it harder.

In the end, I'd failed.

I wonder why Miyuki randomly decided to have me read it? I just don't get it. Was she concerned about the fact that I stuck to text only? I mean, I really enjoy making haiku, creating these works of art. I enjoy the way clipped-out words and unexpected combinations can suddenly create new landscapes. But I get no joy out of expressing myself out loud. Haiku is words, and words are text. Isn't that the essence of it?

I get all embarrassed about having people look at my work, but if they can't see my face, like on Curiosity, I'm fine with it. Beaver's tagging was really embarrassing for me—but the fact that I've never told him to cover them up shows, maybe, that part of me kind of likes it.

"*Don't you think*," Miyuki told me, "*there are some aspects that can only be conveyed when you say them out loud?*"

Maybe, but...

"They come across, okay? Whether you say them out loud or not."

You have to feel it. Sense it. I'm laying it all out in black and white for you, on paper. Or like this.

I pick up my phone and post a comment on Curiosity.

```
Cherry @ Haiku account

Summer's lustrous sheen
There's a false start in the wind
and the evening dusk
#haiku
```

That's good enough for me.

Putting down my phone, I get off my bed and look around the room again.

The bed is half tucked into the bottom part of the closet. When I sleep, I go in there up to my shins. On the upper level of the closet are clothes, storage boxes, and some stationery I no longer use. My desk is set up along the wall at the entrance to the room, but it holds more haiku books than study materials. Dad made it as a DIY project. Some boxes next to it are filled with back issues of *Haiku Monthly*. The bookshelf above the desk contains my textbooks and stuff. On top of that are action figures of the fictional superheroes

I used to like, a daruma figure, an old shoebox, and so on. On the side table by the bed is an alarm clock, and on the wall above it is a haiku calendar with a focus on the more serious classics... Looking at it all makes me realize that I've accumulated a ton of stuff.

Okay. Let's get started. I pick up the cardboard moving boxes that are propped up against the balcony window.

As I am packing my stuff, I hear a faint voice at the front door saying hello. I look at my watch and see that it is a little before seven in the evening. Dad's home early today. "Good evening," comes my mother's loud voice from the dining room.

I leave my room with the boxes I have packed so far. The front door faces my room, so I immediately see Dad untying his leather shoes with a slow, steady hand.

"Dad, can I put this stuff in that room over there?"

I'm referring to Dad's study–slash–storage room.

"Huh? Oh, sure."

Dad nods, so I make my way to the study.

"But aren't you packing too soon? We don't move until next month."

"Oh, I'm sure we'll have a million things to do once the date comes closer. Best to handle what we can right now," Mom suggests wisely.

Dad asked me the question, but Mom replied first, so I leave it at that.

"Sure, right. How's your back? Feeling better?" He switches to questioning Mom.

"Mmm, it's still not a hundred percent...," she says with a wince.

"Well, don't push it. I'll help with chores and stuff."

"Aw, thank you! Could you make breakfast?"

"You know I can't cook."

"But you said you'd help."

"I meant, like, cleaning or grocery shopping."

"That'd be nice, too, but..."

This apartment isn't very big, so I can basically hear everything said inside it.

"Yui," Mom says as I return to my room, "we'll have dinner ready soon."

I respond with a flat, "Okay," and go on my way.

* * *

"I'm coming in."

Dad barges into my room as I continue to organize my stuff. I keep going, not stopping for him.

"Pretty useful saijiki, huh?" He sits on the bed, looking down at my still-open phone case. "I gave that to you, so take good care of it, okay?"

"I know, Dad. I will."

I take down the shoebox atop the bookshelf and check inside. It has old New Year's postcards from my friends, stickers that I used to collect, plus other odds and ends. I put the whole thing as is into a moving box.

"You don't mind moving, do you, Yui?"

"Huh?" I stop and look at Dad. He glances around the room, a can of beer in his hand.

"It just seems like you're cleaning up pretty fast, so…"

Do I mind this…?

"…Anywhere's the same to me," I flatly reply with the truth. "As long as I have my phone…"

"You think?" Dad says as I get back to work. "…Well, thanks for taking over your mother's part-time job for her."

"Sure."

"Just be careful you don't throw *your* back out, too, okay, son?"

"Uh-huh."

"And dinner's ready."

"Oh."

Dad leaves the room as soon as he says that. I stop my work and follow him.

I'm currently subbing in for Mom over at Sunnyside. Mom hurt her back while she was getting an early start on the moving work. Apparently, finding a replacement for her would be a big pain, so since I wasn't in any school clubs or teams, I was offered to serve as an impromptu replacement. It wasn't retail or anything; I'd just be dealing with a bunch of old folks; I figured it'd be easy enough. So I said yes.

"Mom…"

She gives me a "What?" look from the opposite side of the table. Meanwhile,

I take a bite of the *goya champuru* stir-fry we are having for dinner… The taste of the bitter melon really stands out.

"Can you *please* stop liking my posts?"

Having her be the only person liking any of my comments is, in its own way, embarrassing. Really, zero would be a lot better than her one.

"Huh?" Mom puts her chopsticks down. "What for? I'm the only one giving you any likes!" She accents this with a smile and the peace sign… *That's exactly what's embarrassing about it, Mom.*

Ba-ding. I get a notification on my phone, which is on the table. Putting my chopsticks down, I check the screen and am so surprised by what I find that I promptly stand up, fly out of the dining room, and run for my own room, bumping into the fridge and dish rack along the way.

"No phones during dinner," I hear Dad say behind me. But…

[Curiosity]
Smile liked your comment.

"Smile…"

That Smile, right…? I mean, it's a pretty common account name to have, I know…but would any other Smile show up at *this* moment? Like… What the hell?!

Before I can get my head around it, the SMILE LIKED YOUR COMMENT notification bar appears and disappears on my screen, over and over. Launching the Curiosity app, I find that an account named Smile has liked all the haiku I have posted so far. I tap the account name and check out the profile.

Smile For Me!

I'm Smile from Orange Sunshine!
I'm also on Curiolive: check it out!
Followers: 168.391

Orange Sunshine… The group Japan had mentioned. It really *is* that Smile. She gave my haiku a ton of likes, but…is this her way of asking for a follow…?

The FOLLOW button is on the right side of her profile page. Slowly, I move my index finger closer to it...but then stop. What should I do? It'd be *so* embarrassing if I had the wrong idea or something. No but then again, following someone on Curiosity is totally normal...

Then with my momentum getting the better of me, I press the FOLLOW button. I did it... I really did it!

Then another notification.

[Curiosity]
Smile followed you back.

No way...!

I check my follower count and find that, yes, it is now five where it used to be four. Japan, Beaver, Maria ☆, HaikuBot...and Smile. Seriously, she's following me. Like, wasn't that a little *too* fast?

Smile's icon is easy to recognize. It's a big, stylized smiley emoticon, and the way it has its tongue sticking out a little is...

"Cute..."

Oh. I can't help but say it out loud.

"Your voice! I think it's cute!"

Smile's voice echoes in my head again. It was just a series of words, nothing unusual or special, but I find myself thinking them over and over again.

Cute. Cute. A cute voice. I want to hear more of it.

The next thing I know, I was done typing it out. It had flashed through my mind, and now I was about to post it on Curiosity.

Cherry @ Haiku account

All too hard to hear
the owner of the voice that
searches for summer
#haiku

My latest piece appears on the timeline. Mm. I like it.

Oops. There it is again. I can't help but laugh when I see the notification bar on the screen. *Do you really need to be so quick about it?*

[Curiosity]
Smile liked your comment.

My daily life, which had been set and passed by in a huge mall, changed little by little after I met Smile.

My shortcut to the mall through the rice paddy is actually on her family's land, it turns out. We never make any formal plans, but sometimes, if we run into each other after my shift at Sunnyside is over, we take that farm road back home together. She always has a mask on whenever I see her, no matter how hot it is.

Cherry @ Haiku account

It was almost like
you never even cared once
for the shining sun
#haiku

Whenever I am on break from my job, I often pass the time at Kato Books. Today, as usual, I go to the literature section and realize that Smile has beat me there. Taking a closer look, I see that she is taking pictures of something on her phone while talking.

"Do you know this?" she says. "It's called a saijiki. I learned about these just recently; it's like a dictionary for people who write haiku... Huh? Aw, c'mon, it's *so* cute!"

Cherry @ Haiku account

Sunflowers asking
what "cute" means, looking it up
in dictionaries
#haiku

I've checked out her Curiolive stream, too. It is incredibly popular, just like Japan said it was. Not even ten minutes into a broadcast, her viewer count is pushing fifty thousand, the number of comments and likes well into five figures, like it is totally normal for her. Comparing that with my own follower and like counts, I can't help but feel really, really small.

Smile always wears a mask during her streams. I wonder if that bothers her viewers at all. Some of them bring it up in their comments, but Smile never acknowledges them.

So I subscribe to the channel and set up my notifications so I'll know when the streaming starts.

Cherry @ Haiku account

The early sunrise
makes me wonder just how cute
my words truly are
#haiku

The next time I see Smile, it is during one of our mall haiku excursions. She is wearing a mask now, too.

She is with her sisters this time. I saw them once in that video chat—the girl with the glasses and the other with the hair buns. She introduces them to me: Julie is the one with glasses, and the one with the hair buns is Marie.

The three of them are so good at talking and being social. They make fast friends with everyone at Sunnyside. The seniors invite the girls to come on down to the center with them, and (much to my surprise) they actually seem excited about the idea.

As I expected, Nami, Akiko, and Ms. Tanaka all welcome them with open arms. It feels like everyone just loves those three sisters. Ever since then, Smile visits Sunnyside now and then, and that...gives me an excuse to walk home with her more often.

Cherry @ Haiku account

Summer cold, perhaps?
That mask does too good a job
of hiding your smile
#haiku

Japan told me that Smile has been on Curiolive ever since she was little. She was initially popular because her huge buckteeth made her super cute, like a beaver. She was wearing braces the first time I saw her at the mall, and ever since then, Smile has had a mask on whenever I see her. The mask, the teeth, the braces... Clearly, she is getting those popular buckteeth fixed but doesn't want anyone to see or comment about it. That's what it was, I'm sure.

Now I kind of regret muttering, "Braces..." under my breath back then. If she ran away in a panic like that, she must have some serious hang-ups about her mouth. If anything, I think those teeth are unique and charming—maybe she doesn't see it that way at all?

But bringing it up feels like a bad idea.

Cherry @ Haiku account

Amid daylight shade,
all I want to discover
is the true reason
#haiku

Then I realize: All my recent haiku have been inspired by Smile.

I'm unconsciously following Smile with my eyes. Even in her streams, her voice through my headphones sounds totally natural. I want to hear more of her, so whenever I'm with Smile in real life, I have my headphones off.

Before I know it, casually calling her Smile comes totally naturally to me.

And then I realize... I like Smile. When I think about her, I feel the emotions well up. All these words keep on bubbling up. And I know how to express these feelings with words.

Cherry @ Haiku account

Throughout my whole life,
at last I find words bubble
up like soda pop
#haiku

I tear the July sheet off the haiku calendar in my room, revealing August. Today's the first of the month; the heat's still as intense as ever, and the air conditioner's barely doing its job in my room. I bring a finger up to Saturday, the seventeenth.

Movers coming 4 PM.

That's the day we're scheduled to move.

Looking around my room, I see that it is maybe halfway tidy, just like how my AC is halfway functional. I'd begun packing pretty early on, but I haven't really touched it at all lately. Not because I'm busy. I just haven't felt like it.

I pick up the phone on the desk, put my headphones down, and start to head out. As I put my shoes on by the front door, I hear Mom's voice from the dining room.

"Hey, isn't practice for the daruma dance about to start soon?"

"Yeah, today's the first day. I have the song on my phone."

I turn around to find Mom peeking out from the doorway.

"Oh, it's not a CD?"

I shake my head and walk out the door. "Good luck with it!" she shouts at me, her voice echoing through the hot and humid halls of the apartment.

Every year in mid-August, the city of Oda holds a big summer event, the Mt. Oda Daruma Festival. It's well-known to the locals, and the Nouvelle

Mall serves as its venue. The rooftop parking lot becomes the main event space, with a bunch of stalls and people doing the Daruma Ondo dance around this little festival tower. It's been put on since I was a child.

One of the regular events is the fireworks display they shoot off from the rice paddies. It lasts for about an hour, and some of the fireworks are really big, so by local standards it's a pretty large-scale show. A lot of people from neighboring towns come to see them, so the roof of the mall is always packed with spectators.

When I arrive at the mall, I find a large sign placed next to the one Beaver had tagged earlier, which reads 16 DAYS TO GO UNTIL THE 56TH MT. ODA DARUMA FESTIVAL! The number of days is designed to be torn off and replaced, so it'll say 15 DAYS TO GO tomorrow.

Inside, you can see signs here and there that people are prepping for the festival. The banners that hang in the stairwell are being converted to festival-related designs, and most of the stores must be in "get ready for the new season" mode because they are all setting up their own festival decorations. It is kind of a big deal around here.

When I arrive at the Central Court, I am greeted by a large banner announcing the date of the festival.

56TH MT. ODA DARUMA FESTIVAL

SATURDAY, AUGUST 17

5 PM

It is on the seventeenth this year, something they announced before summer vacation began. We'd been talking about it at school, so I already knew. This banner doesn't surprise me at all.

It's just that…there's something else happening that day…

"We're doing the daruma dance again this year, so let's all give it our best shot!"

Ms. Tanaka dances as she calls out to everyone in the room. They all respond, "Yeah!" in unison. Just like I told Mom, today is the start of rehearsals for the dance we'll perform at the Daruma Festival. The "Daruma Ondo" song is playing on a small speaker connected to my phone. All the seniors practice the movements seated while Ms. Tanaka, who stands across from them, directs their dance moves.

Me, Nami, Akiko, and Smile (in a mask) are all in a line, dancing along to the music. Smile has grown to feel quite at home in Sunnyside, and she is joining us for today's practice as well. I heard she invited Julie and Marie to join her, but they are busy, so Smile is the only one here today.

As we dance together—though Akiko is between us—my attention is less on the daruma choreography and more on Smile. Being together with her makes me...happy. Practicing the Daruma Ondo is fun thanks to her.

"I've been thinking about this for a while," Akiko says to Smile, dancing to her right, "but this song is so lame, isn't it?"

"Oh, for sure. Kind of *rustic*, you know?"

"Daruma Ondo" is a major hit with Oda residents. In fact, we've been taught this song and dance since kindergarten. It's so ingrained in everyone's mind that we honestly don't even need to rehearse this. I don't know when this tune was created, but for some reason, it was composed using these cheap-sounding synths, not sounding at all like the traditional Japanese festival piece it is supposed to be.

> Havin' fun in Mt. Oda, land of the rice fields ♪
> Blue sky, spinning donuts, there, there we go! ♪
> The darumas dance and bounce around, look at all of 'em go ♪
> Ahhh, one, two, one, two, one, two, three! ♪

> Get out from the hot spring, put your yukata on ♪
> Discs spin, moon shines, there, there we go! ♪
> The daruma sing and party on, look at all of 'em go ♪
> Ahhh, one, two, one, two, one, two, three! ♪

"What are the 'discs' about?" Akiko asks. "UFOs, or what?"

"Maybe Mt. Oda sees a lot of them... Ah, Nami?!"

Smile suddenly cries out, accompanied by Akiko going "Huhhh?!"

"Ohhh, I can't take this song," sobs Nami from next to me. "It just brings back so many memories..."

When I look at her, I see that she is crying so hard that I have no idea how to react...all while continuing her dancing. Ms. Tanaka and the old folks notice something is wrong, too, and soon, everyone stops.

"What's going on?" Smile asks.

"It was just so...so *pure*, like..."

Nobody prods her about it, but apparently "Daruma Ondo" evokes some pretty nostalgic memories for Nami. What could it be, though...?

After the rehearsal, Nami is back to her usual self as she goes about her business. Smile stays at Sunnyside until five, when my shift ends, chatting and playing games with everyone the whole time. As I'm doing maintenance on the facility's care equipment, I see Nami and Akiko approaching Smile, who is in the middle of a circle of old people. What are they talking about? I am too far away to hear, but I am so curious that I stop my work and look over.

Nami and Akiko put their hands together in front of their chests and bow to Smile. Confused, she waves her hands to stop their bowing. The other two look up at the same time and take Smile's hands in theirs, reasoning with her. Are they asking her for something...?

...Oh. Smile must've said something because now Nami and Akiko are smiling happily. Smile's own expression is...the same. Even with her mask on, the confusion is obvious.

"They offered me a part-time job."

"Huh?"

Smile explains what they'd said while we both walk home. Just like before, we're going along that farm path in the early evening, separated by the ruts.

"But I'm still in high school. I don't have a caregiver license or anything."

"Oh, you don't need one to work at that facility..."

"Right, yeah. Nami told me so, and I guess it makes sense. She said *you* didn't have one, either, so high-school students are no problem at all."

I nod. I heard all about the requirements when I took over for Mom.

"...So what do you think?"

Smile's voice sounds quieter to me now. Looking over, I realize she is watching the ruts on the path as she walks. What is up with that? I'm not sure, but I feel like something about her has changed. Or am I imagining it? I'm not sure. I might get to work with her at Sunnyside... But I'm moving away in almost three weeks. If I'm with Smile, maybe we could talk more about haiku with Mr. Fujiyama? Ohhh, but I can't just use Smile like that...

A rush of feelings comes and goes in a flash. The more aware I become of how much I like Smile, the easier it is for my emotions to spin out of control.

"...Yeah," I whisper softly. A halfhearted response. Not cool at all.

"Uh-huh," she replies, just as softly. Her voice is usually so clear through her mask, but that "uh-huh" was so quiet, I can't guarantee that she actually said it at all.

The ruts slowly disappear behind us. Even with my eyes on the ground like this, the setting sun is almost blinding. The only sounds clinging to my ears are us walking down the farm road and the croaking from the frogs in the rice paddies.

Smile, what kind of face are you making?

Smile, why did your expression change just now?

Smile, are you...picking up on my out-of-control feelings?

Amid daylight shade, all I want to discover is the true reason

"A job, huh?"

After dinner, I go back to my room and lie on my bed, thinking about the part-time job Nami and her friend offered me at Sunnyside. I've never had a job before; Curiolive doesn't allow underage streamers to collect ad revenue, so I'm not getting affiliate money or anything.

Still, I really like being at home. I don't have to wear a mask in here. Talking doesn't dry out my mouth and lips, and I don't have to deal with ear pain from the straps. I know it'd be much easier to go around in public and do my streams like this, but I just can't do it without a mask...

At least Cherry and the other people I've been meeting lately haven't asked me about the mask. That's a relief.

So I roll around on the bed, holding a plushie (a floppy tapir) in my arms like a body pillow. I am on my back, so I'm looking at the ceiling. Cone-shaped purple lace hangs from above, which makes it look kind of like a fantasy landscape; I like staring at it. Sometimes the lace shakes when Marie's deep into some game up in the loft.

On the way home today, I told Cherry about the job offer, but he didn't show much of a reaction. Isn't he interested at all? I took a glance or two at him, but he kept looking down the whole time. Which, I mean, he does that a lot, but...

Maybe I'm mistaken, but I feel like Cherry as of late (not that we've known each other for that long...) is different from when we first met. He used to act all weird about calling me Smile, but now he's totally chill with it. I noticed that right off. He's just acting more...natural now. That makes me feel all warm and fuzzy inside.

Ever since we got friendlier, we've started bumping into each other in the mall more often—by coincidence, I think... Though now that I think of it, it's usually me finding him somewhere, not the other way around... Well, maybe not, actually. That time at the bookstore when I was streaming about this saijiki I found (I remembered the word for it!), he was the one who found me.

Even in Sunnyside, I can kind of feel Cherry's eyes on me...I think. Cherry hangs out with Mr. Fujiyama a lot (his bushy hair is so cute), and when I look toward the sofa where they usually sit, my eyes meet his pretty often... or maybe he's looking at one of the clients instead of me? But it's not like I can just ask him, "Hey, do you look at me a lot?" He'd be so weirded out. It sounds so self-centered.

...I've been acting like this a lot lately. I'm sitting here, thinking about something else, and the next thing I know, my mind's on Cherry.

I roll around on my bed again, sinking into it as I flatten my tapir plush. I take my phone out from under my pillow and tap the Curiosity icon, still lying on my back. Checking my timeline, I find that a lot of people I follow have posted updates.

...Oh.

Cherry @ Haiku account

Summer mountain scents
have full permission to take
my body away
#haiku

A new haiku from Cherry. I can't help but smile when I see it. He never talks much about himself, but whenever one of his poems is written in the first person, I just find that so cute! It's interesting, how he portrays these two different aspects of himself between real life and haiku. When I imagine him talking about himself to me in real life, I just smile more and more...and eventually I laugh so hard, my shoulders shake. Oh, man, Cherry is *so* cute.

So I give the haiku a like and send off a reply.

Smile @ Orange Sunshine

I'm gonna snatch ya!

Cherry's response arrives immediately. I laugh again.

Cherry @ Haiku account

Please

Smile @ Orange Sunshine

Ha-ha-ha! What's that mean?!

And then he pulls back outta nowhere. Ha-ha-ha! But I can kind of imagine the face he's making. Maybe a little unsure of himself...

"What's up, Yuki?"

"You're kinda scaring us..."

Julie and Marie, studying at the table we share, are staring right at me.

"He wanted to be snatched away by me," I replied. They both give me quizzical looks...and it's so hilarious that I can't stop laughing.

After that, he and I talk via DM (for the first time, come to think of it).

Cherry is chattier than when we talk in real life. The conversation goes on and on, and before I know it, a whole hour has gone by. It is *so* much fun. Definitely a little different from the conversations I have with viewers in Curiolive. This feels like something more secret, somehow.

By the time I type *good night* and get out of bed, Marie is gone, and all I see is Julie studying at our table.

"Julie, you had a part-time job last year, right? At the mall?"

"Yeah. I quit to focus on college prep, though. Why?"

"Did you tell Mom and Dad about it first?"

"Well, yeah. The store needed their signatures and stuff."

"Okay. I'll talk with them, too, then!"

"So here's our new friend starting today…"

"Say hello to Smile!"

"Great to have you here!"

Nami and Akiko loudly introduce me to the usual gang, and I bow as low as I can in response. Cherry, Ms. Tanaka, and all the clients applaud me, which is nice to see.

I wound up accepting the offer from Sunnyside. I am a little nervous, since this is no longer a casual hangout for me, but I know everybody here already. I'm sure it'll be fine.

The staff at Sunnyside all wear the same pink polo shirts and name badges around their necks. Nami writes *Smile* ♡ on my badge. I think that's a little embarrassing…but also pretty cute. It kinda feels like someone on Curiolive giving my stream a heart, except in real life.

My job is the same as Cherry's—basically supporting Nami and the full-timers. While they are busy with work, I talk with the seniors, play games with them, watch TV with them, and so on.

After a few days of working at Sunnyside, I think I now know a little bit more about assisting the elderly. I even learn some seated exercises. I'll teach them to my grandpa next time I see him.

I also go on their haiku excursions (which I learned is a fancy word meaning *walk* or *stroll*). We stroll around the mall, find a subject, and write a haiku about it…but I'm terrible at writing haiku! It reminds me all over again about how amazing Cherry is. It turns out that Miyuki, the woman with the long black hair, really *is* a haiku teacher. She's super kind and beautiful, and I'm a little envious of how mature she seems.

During our excursions (and sometimes just at random, too), there have been a few times when Mr. Fujiyama wanders off, and Cherry and I have to search for him. "He's usually in the mall," Cherry says, "so he's not too hard to find"—and usually he'll be found inside somewhere, but occasionally he'll go outside, too. He was up on the rooftop parking lot the other day. I was worried he'd suffer from sun exposure, but fortunately, he was just fine.

Anyway, whenever Mr. Fujiyama goes for one of his walks, I try to find him as soon as possible. I asked Nami about the record he carries around— I've been wondering about that square bit of cardboard Mr. Fujiyama takes great care of—and she told me it is a record jacket.

I wasn't sure working part-time was really for me at first, but once I started, I found it to be a lot of fun. I think most people take jobs like these just for the money, but I'm so comfortable interacting with the people at Sunnyside. Unlike Curiolive streams, it is refreshing to communicate with so many people I can see face-to-face and to interact with people of all ages, for that matter.

Most of all, though, I'm glad I can get to know Cherry better. Whenever we work the same shift, we always go home together. I never explicitly offered to, and neither did he. We just kinda did it. Totally natural.

"Toughboy isn't here, is he?"

The clock at Sunnyside has just ticked past five in the afternoon, so I think it is a good time to ask Nami that. This is around the time Mr. Fujiyama's grandson, Toughboy, (I wonder what his real name is?) comes stomping in, and whenever he sees Akiko, he starts grinning and talking nonsense to himself. It's so silly. To me, he functions as kind of a timer to tell me my shift is almost over, but for some reason he hasn't shown up yet.

Nami sighs, a little disgusted. "He never shows up when Akiko's working the early shift. That little weirdo is so *obvious* with it."

Akiko worked the morning shift today and left about two hours before we arrived.

Nami approaches Mr. Fujiyama, who is sitting on the sofa. "Okay, Mr. Fujiyama," she says softly, "you'll be taking the van back home today!"

"Hohh." Mr. Fujiyama nods.

"Cherry, Smile... The van should be waiting behind the mall, so can you take him over there for me?"

Cherry and I briskly finish wiping down the tables, and then the three of us head for the employee entrance. Nami says we can head straight home after escorting Mr. Fujiyama, so I punch my time card and change into my normal clothes.

We step outside and discover a pretty blue-to-orange gradient sky. Something I didn't realize before I started working at the mall is that the building has no windows at all, so it's hard to get a sense of the passage of time. I asked Cherry about it, and he said, "Yeah, I guess so." Maybe he doesn't pick up on that as much?

Outside, the Sunnyside van is waiting for us, just as Nami said. The driver (who says he drives for a lot of day-service facilities like ours) opens the door for us; Mr. Fujiyama and I sit in the back, and Cherry gets the passenger seat. Nobody else needs transport today, so we head straight for Mr. Fujiyama's place.

"Okay, off we go," the driver says, starting the van without having to ask where we are going.

The van drives down the main road near the mall. Outside the window, the shimmering summer light (another phrase Cherry taught me) is streaming by us. I look at Mr. Fujiyama sitting next to me, staring at the record jacket on his lap.

"Here we are!"

I look outside. I actually know this place. It's a line of shops just a short walk from my house. Mr. Fujiyama lives pretty close to me; in fact, I can walk home from here easily, so I tell the driver that we'll be getting out as well.

When I get out of the van, I find a small one-story building that looks like it had been a prefab job. On the roof is a sign vaguely shaped like a mountain.

"Fujiyama…Records?"

The sign says Fujiyama Records. So it's a record store? The building looks pretty worn down, and I can easily imagine this store getting no customers at all—something likely true for the other shops along this street, actually.

Mr. Fujiyama slowly walks away, going up to the sliding door that serves as the store entrance. There is a sign with Closed written on it hanging from the door, but he flips it around. It bangs against the glass of the door a bit; the other side reads Open. Then Mr. Fujiyama rattles the door open and goes inside.

The moment we follow him in, we are greeted with an unusual scent. Even with the mask on, I pick up on it right away. A mix of dust and old paper… I feel like I've smelled something like this before, and then I recognize it: the smell of the shed where we keep our farm equipment.

Mr. Fujiyama walks to the back of the store, not bothering to turn on the lights, and sits down on a chair behind the counter. I slowly make my way through the darkened store space.

"Wow… What *is* this?"

I can't help but ask. The space is about the size of a small café or a spacious living room. Along the walls are racks much taller than I am, and on the racks are record jackets (that's what they call them, right?) all packed tight with zero room to fit anything else. The wall of racks alone is an overwhelming sight, but in the middle of the store, three long tables are laid out parallel to one another, and there is only enough space between them for maybe one person to pass. On top of them are cardboard boxes, filled to the brim with even more record jackets. There are T-shirts and posters near the entrance, too, and next to the counter are a fan and square box that looks like a refrigerator, but otherwise the place is nothing but records. That must be the source of the unique smell that permeates the place.

The jackets on the racks are shelved so that you can see the spines, so I can read what I guess are the titles.

Moanin' in the Moonlight (Howlin' Wolf)
NEU! (NEU!)
Crazy Rhythms (The Feelies)

*   *   *

I don't know any of the names. For that matter, my English isn't good enough to even read them. Are these non-Japanese bands? I peek into the cardboard boxes on the tables; inside are a lot more record jackets, although they are a little smaller than the ones on the racks. Guess they come in a bunch of different sizes.

I pick up a few of them.

Here Come the Judge (Pigmeat Markham)
Superrappin' (Grandmaster Flash & The Furious Five)

...Still not ringing any bells.

I look at Cherry, only to find that he has pulled out one of the record jackets from a box. He puts his hand in the jacket and pulls out the contents, revealing a black disc—a record.

"Are these *all* records...?" Cherry seems overwhelmed.

"Is this your first time here?"

He has been working at Sunnyside far longer than me, so I sort of assumed he'd come here a few times before.

"The first time going in," Cherry says, putting the record back in its box. I see. No wonder he's in a state of shock.

"This record... I've listened to it the most out of anything."

Mr. Fujiyama's voice echoes in the dimly lit store. He is sitting at the counter, staring at that record jacket he always holds on to.

"Over...and over..."

He sounds really lonely. I walk closer to them. Cherry seems to think this is unusual behavior for Mr. Fujiyama. He slowly begins to walk over, and I follow.

"I...want to hear it again."

When we get to the counter, I can see Mr. Fujiyama's shoulders shaking.

"If I could hear it again...I could remember..."

"...Remember what?" I ask, bending my knees a bit to make eye contact.

"I don't want to forget...but I can't remember..."

It isn't quite functioning as a conversation. His shaky voice makes my heart ache. He has this record he cherishes so much, and he believes that if he hears it, it'll help him recall something. But he has no idea where it is, and he keeps looking and looking, but to no avail…

"I can't remember…"

Tears begin to fall from his tired, downtrodden eyes. I find myself rushing to Mr. Fujiyama's side, hugging him around his shoulders. When he looks at me, another tear spills out, and I almost start crying myself. He slowly holds his record jacket out to me. I fight back my tears and take it.

"Thank you."

I stand up and examine it with Cherry, who has come to my side. This is my first close-up look at it. Having it in my hands, I'm surprised at its size. It is a square paper jacket about the size of two school notebooks. The front has a pink background with a white circle in the middle the size of your palm. Surrounding the circle, on the top half, is some text:

"*YAMAZAKURA…*"

The word *yamazakura*, or mountain cherry blossom, is written in a bold font. Is this the title…? I tilt the jacket a bit, discovering that the circle is actually a little uneven. I touch it with my hand.

"Oh, it's a hole…"

The white circle is actually just a hole. It looks white because that's the color of the inner cardboard.

I turn the jacket over to look at the other side.

"Aw, cute…"

Again, I can't help but say it. The other side is a photo of a line of cherry blossoms and…a big electrical tower, I guess? But what draws my attention is the woman standing there. She is probably around twenty, with long, poofy hair, a flower-patterned dress, and an English-style flat cap. It must have been a windy day because she has a hand over the cap so it doesn't fly off. She has this cute, kind of bashful smile, and the way her floral dress flutters along with the cherry blossoms in the wind adds to her smile. You don't see this kind of fashion these days. It's probably an old record—maybe this look was more popular a while back?

One more thing makes me curious. The woman's smiling with her mouth wide open, and something really big sticks out from there. She has buckteeth. But she's so cute, too…

I bring the jacket closer to my face to examine it in detail, as if peering through a microscope. Then my gaze falls on the side of the jacket. Something is poking out of it a little, a piece of paper about as wide as my little finger. I grab it and pull it out of the jacket. It is longer than I expected—as long as the jacket, in fact. It is a really flimsy piece of paper, cut into a strip that is meant to go around the jacket, it seems. It is folded, and when I turn it over, I see a part of the photograph from the back cover, along with a number that I assume was the price.

"What's this thing?"

I hand it to Cherry. Some kind of bonus to go with the record? I don't know enough about this stuff.

"*Sakura petals, they fade on the wind without…*"

Cherry's voice is at a whisper.

"*…a word of farewell.*"

He is chewing through each word. I don't know what he is talking about, but when I look sideways at the strip of paper I handed him, I finally understand. That sentence is printed vertically on the paper strip—*Sakura petals, they fade on the wind without a word of farewell.*

"*…A haiku?*"

The five-seven-five rhythm is clearer when Cherry says it, but he doesn't answer the question. His expression becomes even sterner than before.

"*Sakura petals, they fade on the wind without a word of farewell.*"

Now he is speaking even more softly than before, almost like he's talking to himself.

Something feels odd to me this time. The intonation of the word *sakura* isn't like before. The first time around, it was *sakura* as in cherry blossoms, but this time it feels more like *Sakura*, his name.

Cherry still looks kind of gloomy; now doesn't seem like a good time to ask him questions. His head is down, eyes closed, and he is totally silent. Around him is the same invisible barrier I'd felt when we first walked home together. I'm really curious about the "sakura" thing, but I can't ask about it...

The small store feels stifling now, like it is caving in on us. I wait patiently for Cherry's next words.

"...I'm gonna look for it."

He says it quietly but forcefully, like he is releasing all his breath at once. Then he looks up and shows the strip of paper to Mr. Fujiyama.

"I'll look for your record, too, Mr. Fujiyama!"

His voice is clear and penetrating as he makes the declaration. He wants Mr. Fujiyama to be completely sure of his intentions, I suppose—and as I listen next to him, his voice, and every word he says, resonates in my heart. My body is heated up. His desires come across to me, crystal clear.

I take another look at the woman on the jacket. She is smiling brightly, like her buckteeth are the last thing on her mind.

"...I want to play it for him, too," I say, the words coming easy to me. My emotions are spilling over. "I want Mr. Fujiyama to remember what was so important to him."

I hold the jacket to my chest as I look at Mr. Fujiyama. He is looking back at me, tears not dried yet. His eyes are slightly open, and I wonder if he can sense our intentions.

When I look at Cherry, the barrier has gone away and he is smiling at me. He's so kind like that. He's really doing his best for Mr. Fujiyama. I want to look for it with him, too. *I'll join you, Cherry. I'll do whatever it takes!*

Whump!

I turn toward the loud noise—and suddenly, the blood drains from my face. Mr. Fujiyama is slumped over the counter.

"Mr. Fujiyama!"

I immediately run up and shake him by the shoulder. He doesn't respond. Maybe he is unconscious. No matter how many times I call out to him, he never answers.

"...Dad!"

I hear a cry from the doorway. Looking over, I see a short-haired woman, who appears to be just a little older than my mother, rushing toward me.

Cherry and I move a little away from Mr. Fujiyama, as if pushed off by her momentum. I am kind of floored by it all, and Cherry and I just wind up watching as she takes care of Mr. Fujiyama.

Mr. Fujiyama's house is located behind the store. Cherry and I help carry him back. Then while the paramedics are looking at him, Cherry calls Sunnyside to explain what happened. "Ms. Tanaka and Nami will be here later," he says as he ends the call. "They said we could go home for now."

Maybe they did, but after the paramedics leave, Cherry and I kind of hang out by the front door, not really sure what we should be doing. After a while, the woman who discovered Mr. Fujiyama comes to us and smiles gently.

"Thanks very much to you both."

She tells me her name is Tsubaki. I guess she's Mr. Fujiyama's daughter; she's dressed in kind of an eccentric outfit with some stylish glasses, both of which suit her perfectly.

"So you're Toughboy's mother?" Cherry asks.

"Yes." She nods. "You really *do* call Yasuyuki 'Toughboy,' huh?"

"Um, so how's Mr. Fujiyama...?"

"They said it's a mild case of heatstroke. They gave him an IV drip, but he wasn't bad off enough to merit a trip to the ER, so they told me to give him plenty of bed rest at home."

"Oh, good..."

Well, at least Mr. Fujiyama is doing all right.

"I'm sorry, I..." Cherry holds his head down. "I should have...been with him on his walks more often..."

It *has* been very hot lately. I suppose Cherry feels responsible for letting Mr. Fujiyama go on his little strolls all the time.

"I couldn't find him very quickly, either, though..."

It's not just your fault, Cherry.

"It's all right," Tsubaki says, smiling and shaking her head. "He's not suffering or anything like that, so...you know."

She is showing real concern for us. That makes her words even more painful.

"Um, Tsubaki..." I hand her the jacket I still have in my hands. "I guess he's looking for a record that's really important to him. He wants to hear it again..."

Tsubaki stares at the jacket, quietly listening to my story.

"He's looking all around the mall for it, too, so..."

She looks at us. She is smiling, but she seems kind of troubled, or sad. Instead of replying, she looks at the jacket again. Looking at that inscrutable expression, I decide it is wiser not to dive in any further—and in the end, we leave without learning any more about the record.

It is already night. The farm road doesn't have any lights, so it gets really dark at night. You can easily trip and fall if you aren't careful.

"...I hope Mr. Fujiyama's okay."

As I walk home with Cherry, I find my heart racing, my head full of worry for the old man. I think Cherry feels the same way. I've been trying to chat with him on the way home, but all he says back is "Yeah," then silence. I am taking the lead along the farm path, Cherry following behind, and his voice is almost drowned out by all the frogs in the paddies.

I pull my phone out of my pocket and tap the photo app. I took some pictures of the record jacket before giving it back to Tsubaki—the front, the back, and that other strip of paper.

"You think maybe the record Mr. Fujiyama's looking for is in that store somewhere?"

It seems pretty likely, given all the records in there. But...

"Well, if so, why would he constantly be looking for it around the mall?"

I can see the mall still, all lit up beyond the rice fields. Mr. Fujiyama was definitely looking for it in and around that mall. Is it over there after all?

...Well, no point dwelling on it. I have to take action. I look back at Cherry, walking backward.

"I'll try researching it on my phone."

I'm talking to Cherry, but he keeps his head down.

"We'll probably find out a lot about it. Maybe we can buy another copy, even?"

"Yeah."

Oh, good, he's answering me. But his voice is as low as always, his face still looking down at the ground.

"And Marie knows a lot about this stuff, too. I'll ask her to help once I get home."

"I'll poke around, too."

Finally, he's looking at me. Great.

"Perfect!"

I nod at him, still walking backward. I've walked down this farm road with Cherry many times now, but seeing him from the front like this is kinda strange... He doesn't have *those* on his head today, either.

"By the way, you haven't been wearing them lately, huh?"

I put my hands over my ears to simulate a pair of headphones. Yes, I noticed. He's been going around without them a lot lately.

Cherry's eyes widen in surprise. Then he quickly looks away and whispers something. All the frog croaking around us is so loud, I can't be quite sure what he said, but I definitely made out the last part:

"...and I don't need them anyway."

Need them? What's he mean by that?

So I simply reply, "Okay," and don't ask any more questions.

I adore the leaves
that you hid in and out of
the mountain blossoms

Sakura petals, they fade on the wind without a word of farewell.

As I am busy packing for the move, I think about the meaning behind those words. It is a haiku, for sure, written on a piece of paper inside Mr. Fujiyama's record jacket. It must have something to do with the record he lost...but who could have written it?

...a word of farewell—who does it not say good-bye to? Or couldn't it? And *without*—something went unsaid. There's a clear, assertive tone here.

Sakura petals, they fade on the wind... The petals are flying in the air, spreading away from one another. But why use *sakura* instead of *cherry blossoms* or whatever? For visual effect? Because it's cuter? No... Some kind of double meaning? With what?

My hands stop stuffing my haiku books into the cardboard box. My thoughts are occupying more of my attention. Going off. Dancing high in the sky, these...sakura. Imagery of separation.

The moment I saw that haiku at Fujiyama Records, something about "saying good-bye" made me instantly superimpose my own situation over the haiku. I can picture it in my mind—a storm of cherry petals flying far off into the horizon. From "fade" to "farewell"—a reference to death? ...Or separation.

They don't bother to say good-bye...and I can't tell her I'm moving. I was going to tell Smile on the way home today, but...you know...I didn't think she'd bring up the headphones, and all.

I look at my desktop. At the far end are the headphones I've mostly abandoned there lately. I don't think I've touched them in the past week. Smile must've noticed all along that I didn't have them on... It made me feel a pang in my chest just now. It's a little painful, but I'm more glad about it than anything, sort of.

...Who cares about packing? I pick up my phone and lie down on my bed, opening the browser and searching for *yamazakura record. Sakura petals, they fade on the wind without a word of farewell*. The poem just feels like it was meant for me...and the moment that occurred to me, Mr. Fujiyama and his record no longer seemed like just his problem. I want to find it for him so badly—not just for him, but for me, too. I've got to hear it.

"I thought it'd be easy to find on the internet, but..."

The disappointment in Smile's voice seems to seep out from her mask. We are working the same shift the next day, and as we clock in at the employee entrance, we report back to each other about our progress.

Smile had checked out all the new and used record shops on the net. "You can even buy rare stuff on the net," she says, "right? So I thought maybe we could find it online without having to ransack Mr. Fujiyama's shop for it. But I couldn't find it anywhere. There wasn't even anything on the classified ad sites."

I was pretty disappointed, too. Whether it was on sale somewhere or not, I figured it would show up on a record collector's blog or something like that, but there was just nothing at all out there.

"Right, so listen to this!"

Smile's voice brightens up.

"That cute girl in the photo stuck out to me, so I did an image search using that pic!"

Ah... Yes. A classic Smile move if I ever saw one.

"I don't see any young people wearing the kind of outfit she has on, so I figure it was from a while ago, but apparently it was 'in,' like, fifty years ago."

"So the 1970s?"

"Yeah. So you know, I figured it'd mean, like..."

"That's around when the record was made?"

"Yeah, I thought so, too!"

Smile nods broadly as we walk down Central Court toward Sunnyside.

"Mr. Fujiyama, huh?"

"He doesn't like to talk about himself much…"

While we are on duty, me and Smile decide to ask everyone at Sunnyside about Mr. Fujiyama. Tsubaki had informed the care center that he'd be taking some time off from his visits, out of an abundance of caution.

"I heard he used to work here," Mr. Genda says, resting his chin on his hand.

Huh? Here?

"At the mall?" Smile asks, puzzled.

She must've been thinking the same thing.

"No, no," Mr. Sasaki says, waving his hands. "Before this mall was built."

"Yeah," chimes in Mr. Hyoudou from the other table. "There used to be a big factory on this land."

A factory, huh?

"What kind of factory?" Smile asks.

"It was a vinyl pressing plant. They manufactured records."

"Records…"

The term makes both of us gasp. We didn't have any proof yet, but I have a feeling that it's connected somehow.

"I think," Mr. Genda says, "there's a historical exhibition about Oda's history going on at Nouvelle Hall, right?"

"No, no," Mr. Sasaki replies, "it's more of a photo exhibition."

Smile and I decide to visit it during our lunch break.

FROM A VINYL PRESS TO A SHOPPING MALL, IN PHOTOS—CELEBRATING THE RELEASE OF THE NEW PHOTO BOOK, NOUVELLE MALL: A HISTORY

Nouvelle Hall's entrance is on the second floor, behind a dentist's office; the big poster they put up next to it made it pretty easy to spot. So it's just a history of Nouvelle Mall, then, not the city of Oda? Huh.

The hall is quite spacious—about four times the size of Sunnyside. A bunch of photos are displayed on partitions, presumably the ones they published in that new book, and it is pretty neat to look at them in chronological order.

"That's our rice fields!" Smile points to a large, familiar-looking rice field in one photo. "This is from before I was born, I think. It hasn't changed at all."

She's right. The paddies, and the ridges of Mt. Oda, are pretty much the same as they are now; the only difference is the smaller number of houses around. Some color photos also show the record factory, depicting large trucks entering the huge box-shaped building, employees operating large machines, and other old-timey scenes.

"This machine..." Smile focuses on another photo. "I feel like...I've seen it before."

The picture shows a large green metallic machine, an employee standing beside it holding a black disc that looks like a record.

"Yes," the woman manning the exhibition tells us, "that's a record-pressing machine." She is good at her job, providing us all kinds of information about the factory and subsequent mall.

"Once the factory closed down twenty-eight years ago, the Nouvelle company purchased both the land and the factory on it. Nouvelle builds and operates large-scale commercial sites across Japan, and they transformed the factory into a shopping mall, you see. When Nouvelle builds a large site like this, they make sure they don't completely erase the memory of what was there before, out of respect for the local community. Sometimes they use what was on-site for other purposes, or sometimes they use them to create a monument. I understand that over in the Kansai region, they built a mall over an old baseball stadium and kept the main grandstand intact inside it. In much the same way, this used to be a vinyl plant, so sometimes the clocks and other things you see around the mall are actually records."

I listen silently to the lecture, appreciating it. I didn't expect that kind of history.

"Do you know the big machine with daruma figures on it over on the Southern Court? That's actually a record-pressing machine that used to be in this factory. It's the same model as the one in that picture."

"Oh! Now I remember!"

Smile's eyes widen in recognition.

"So it's not a daruma-making machine after all, huh?"

"No, no," the guide says with a laugh. "It's a memory from this land, you could say. And so is the Daruma Festival."

"It is?" Smile asks.

"Yes, the Daruma Festival originally began as an event held for the employees at the plant. Nouvelle worked with the Oda city government to keep it going after the place was converted to a mall."

"I see…"

"We have a display of festival posters from past years, so make sure you take a look at that as well."

The posters from older Mt. Oda Daruma Festivals are on a wall a short distance away from the main display. There are quite a few.

"Oh, there were fireworks from the very first year?"

Smile looks pretty interested in the posters.

"They launched them from the rice paddies, just like now."

Just like she said, the poster has an aerial photograph of fireworks being shot up from the rice fields. A large factory is also visible in the shot, all lit up attractively by the show. I assume that was the vinyl plant.

"This year is the fifty-sixth festival," Smile continues, turning toward me. "It's been going on for over fifty years…and it started in the 1970s."

She's talking to herself, the elements connecting in her head. The clothing she tracked down using image search, the vinyl plant, the Daruma Festival and its fireworks, the association with the '70s, the fact Mr. Fujiyama used to work here… It all had to be more than a coincidence.

"Someone who used to work at the record press…?"

Ex-Princess looks around at the security guards, a bit flustered. We happened to run into them as we passed by their office, so we thought we'd try asking them.

"Do you guys know anyone?"

The guards all shake their heads.

"I'm on temporary assignment here from the hotel in Naeba," Ex-Princess apologetically states, "so I don't know much about local stuff…"

"Actually," one of the guards says, "have you been to the Hand Off on the third floor?" He points upward.

"No," Smile says.

"They sell used records there, don't they? Maybe they'll have that one you showed me on your phone."

"We don't have any record called *Yamazakura*, no."

"Oh…"

Smile scowled.

Japan happens to be on duty at Hand Off that day, so we have him look into it. But there are no copies in their inventory. It isn't even in the company's database.

"Oh, but wait!"

The loud, sudden outburst makes me recoil a bit. Sometimes not having my headphones is kind of a pain.

"Maybe it's a picture disc!"

Japan rushes to the back of the store, then returns with a record-like disc that he puts on the counter.

"Something like this!"

"Aw, that's cute!"

"Yeah, isn't it?!"

The record Japan brought has a large heart-shaped hole in the jacket, Hikarun smiling through it. When Japan takes it out, we see that Hikarun's picture is printed in full color on the disc itself.

"They call these picture discs. It's kind of a special-edition thing!"

"Oh? Is it a record? Even with the photo on it?"

"It sure is! It works just like one. This is a limited-edition Hikarun release. Artists and idols these days do a lot of online, subscription-based streaming, but sometimes they'll sell this analog vinyl—I mean records, that is—to their fans as a bonus. We're kind of experiencing a new vinyl boom right now, so sometimes you see stuff like this go on sale!"

Japan always acts oddly excited around Smile.

"With picture discs, the record itself becomes part of the design, so that's why there's often a hole in the jacket so you can see what's inside. The jacket you showed me had a big hole in the middle, too, so…"

"I see…"

I'm pretty impressed. Just like Japan said, considering the hole in Mr. Fujiyama's jacket, there is a good chance that it's a picture disc.

"You're amazing, Japan!"

Guess Smile agrees with me.

"Thanks so much!"

I guess Japan's knowledge and deductive reasoning impressed her just as much.

"Awww, ha-ha-ha-ha…"

Smiling bashfully, Japan begins talking to himself, blabbing on about more esoteric record knowledge. I don't really have any idea what he is talking about.

"Whatcha up to? Treasure hunting?"

Beaver peeks out from under the counter. Since when was he in here?

"Something like that," I replied.

"Whoa, really?! Lemme join you!"

He is so weirdly excited. That's Beaver for you—and Japan, too. They get so worked up over stuff like this.

"Right, so I'm looking for a certain record right now, and I was wondering if any of you guys know anyone who could help…"

That night, as I lie in bed, I watch Smile's live stream on my phone. Her voice is beaming through my headphones, which I haven't worn in a while.

Mr. Fujiyama's record jacket appears on the screen. I think these are the pictures Smile took with her phone. "This is the one," she says, switching between the front and rear shots. "I've done a lot of research on it, but anyone have any idea where it's from?"

Hmm, I've never seen this before.

I dunno!

Cute girl on the back.

I don't know.

Mmmm, no idea.

Looks old.

No leads here. The viewers don't seem to have any clue, either.

"Ahhh, too bad…"

Smile's expression sours in disappointment.

I put my phone down on my chest and stare at the white ceiling. Guess we aren't gonna crack this nut that easily. An asset like Japan is a lot rarer than I thought.

"Mt. Umafuse?"

Suddenly, Smile speaks through my headphones again. What I see in the comment box amazes me.

Isn't this one of the electrical towers on Mt. Umafuse?

The guy must've been referring to the tower on the back of the cover, looming behind the woman Smile described as cute.

Oh, right…

In the south side of Oda?

I know it! It's a great spot to view mountain cherry blossoms.

Yeah, the view's super awesome.

That seems to jog the viewers' memories. Mt. Umafuse. It's in Oda, apparently, but down south, huh…? We live on the north side and it's a whole other school district down there, so I never knew. But a great spot for mountain cherry blossoms…?

Once her stream ends, Smile immediately DMs me. She seems just as interested in this place as I am, so we work out a plan and decide to visit Mt. Umafuse together.

Monday, August 12

Mt. Umafuse is in a remote village south of the main city, going up around 1,600 feet above sea level. It's counted as part of the Oda mountain range, but the range itself extends out a pretty long way, so I have no idea which peak is Mt. Umafuse from where I live.

Taking a train and then a bus, we walk up the mountain for about twenty minutes from the bus stop at the base. Unlike the smell of the rice paddies, the scent of earth and leaves in the mountains makes the humid air feel kind of refreshing. Smile seems to enjoy the hike up the mountain, too. We live in a really flat area, so we don't usually hike up mountain paths like this.

Once we are past the trail, we come to a wide gravel road with rows of trees along both sides. The cityscape of Oda spreads out between them, looking kind of like a diorama. I recall that someone said this was a good place for viewing mountain cherry blossoms. I look at the trunk of one tree and see that it has a name tag on it reading *Yamazakura*. And that's exactly what this was—a line of mountain cherry trees.

"Beautiful," Smile murmurs as she looks up at them. I nod back. It is summer now so nothing is in bloom, but the sun shining through the leaves of this dark green canopy above us is pretty in its own way.

So we walk slowly up the road, admiring the trees.

"Oh, there it is!"

Smile stops and points at a steel tower visible through a gap in the tree branches. We run toward it.

It turns out to be an Oda FM radio tower.

Up close, it is huge—or tall, anyway. As tall as the water tower by my apartment complex.

"It's the same one, isn't it?"

Smile shows me her phone. A photo of Mr. Fujiyama's record jacket is on the screen, and the only difference between it and our vantage point is that the cherry blossoms aren't in bloom.

"They definitely took it here."

"Seems right."

I nod and look around. We aren't at the summit yet; the rows of cherry trees still extend ahead of us.

"Huh?"

At the end of this tunnel of green, about fifty yards ahead, I noticed something odd.

"What's that?"

I point it out for Smile.

"A...castle?"

It looks a bit like the keep of an old Japanese castle.

"...What's a castle doing here?" Smile wonders.

The mysterious castle is located at the top of Mt. Umafuse.

Once the rows of cherry trees peter out, the summit is home to a large park, complete with an observation deck and asphalt parking lot. A three-story castle keep is in the middle. It's about as tall as my apartment building, and it isn't very big, either—basically a slightly larger version of a regular single-family house. There are no visitors except for us, and an old man who seems to be in charge is cleaning up around the castle.

The inside is very modern, not at all like an old castle. The concrete walls are covered with framed artwork and posters. Near the entrance, there is a sign carved in wood that reads Mt. Sangou Castle Ruins. It feels more like a classroom display than anything else.

The first floor is an exhibition room with a map of the area around Mt. Umafuse and a big sign on the wall reading Yoshida, City of Oda—Mt. Umafuse Artifacts. Along the walls, and right in the middle of the room as well, are fancy glass cases filled with stuff. We look around a bit, feeling like we are on a field trip. There are *manju* steamed buns that I guess are a local specialty, crystal-like stones and, for some reason, gears built for cars.

Suddenly, I see some long hair out of the corner of my eye—it is Smile's. It smells like sweet flowers...or maybe shampoo...but it sure is close. My heartbeat immediately accelerates. I reflexively turn away; it feels so incredibly hot. I give Smile a sideways glance. She is staring intently into a glass case. I guess she isn't aware. My thoughts are starting to go in a negative direction.

Trying to distract myself, I go over to another case, this one on the opposite side of the room from Smile... Hmm?

"Hey..." I speak up after a piece of black-and-white newsprint catches my attention.

"Hey, look at this..." I tap Smile on the shoulder.

"Yeah?"

She reads the article.

"...This is it!"

She turns to me. I nod vigorously as she takes out her phone and snaps a picture through the glass, the sound of her shutter echoing off the concrete.

"...Singer-songwriter and Oda local Sakura Fujiyama (22)'s new album, *Yamazakura*, features Oda FM's radio tower on the jacket, framed by the famed mountain cherry blossoms of Mt. Umafuse."

Smile reads out the news story from her phone. The top of the article shows a woman in a flower-patterned dress with a big smile on her face. In her right hand is a square board, about twelve inches wide, with a white circle in the middle, YAMAZAKURA printed around it. It is a jacket we know well—the exact same one Mr. Fujiyama has.

The moment I find this piece, I get so excited that I forget about pretty much everything else. It is like finding a treasure map or something.

We hurry over to the observation deck, as if we are hiding some secret from the world and have to avoid detection.

There are some other things in this article that catch my attention. The woman is holding Mr. Fujiyama's record jacket in her right hand, but in her left is a black disc, apparently a record.

"Cherry, is this...?"

Smile looks at me. It's true. That woman's smile is printed right on the disc, just as it appears in this newspaper article. We saw something similar in design just a few days ago at Hand Off.

"Like what Japan said..."

"Yeah. I think it's a picture disc."

The so-called new album was a picture disc, a unique one...but it was definitely a record. It exists now—we are sure of it. The record Mr. Fujiyama wants to find exists, and now we've got our biggest clue yet.

And that isn't the only one.

"This woman's family name..."

I look at Smile. She must've arrived at the same conclusion. She nods, eyes full of conviction.

* * *

"Mom…" Tsubaki speaks softly, the excitement clear in her voice. She picks up the copy of the article we'd printed out from Smile's phone at the convenience store, reading it with a kind smile on her face.

We had come straight down from Mt. Umafuse to Mr. Fujiyama's house that evening. We spent the day gathering the clues, and once we connected the dots, it led us right back here. I thought Mr. Fujiyama might remember something if he saw this article, but he still needs to rest and I don't want to stress him out, so I have Tsubaki take a look instead.

"Where did you get this?"

Smile tells her how we found it.

"If she's your mother…is she Mr. Fujiyama's wife, then?"

Tsubaki gently nods at the question.

"She's very pretty."

"Isn't she?" Tsubaki beams.

"Which means she's Toughboy's grandmother…"

Another nod. "Yasuyuki never got to see her, so I don't think he'd realize it…and I guess I hardly would, either. We don't have many pictures."

Oh? So is she…?

"I've never seen this article before now. I guess Mom really *was* a musician for a while."

"May I ask…where she is now?"

I can't help but ask.

"She passed away from illness soon after giving birth to me. It was before I formed any memories at all, so I know practically nothing about her."

I saw that coming. But…

"Oh… I'm sorry."

Maybe I shouldn't have asked.

"It's all right," Tsubaki replies softly.

We follow Tsubaki to the record store. She stops in front of the entrance facing the street, just like the other day. It is getting dark, the old streetlights shining brightly on the road.

Tsubaki is looking at the FUJIYAMA RECORDS sign up on the roof.

"He said he opened this store so he could sell Mom's records."

Smile looks up at it, too. "Oh, he did?"

"But...actually, we're going to close it up next week."

We both look at Tsubaki.

"It's such an old place, and we don't have anyone who can take over..." Tsubaki's face clouds a little, a twinge of sadness crossing it. "Yasuyuki's in the process of cleaning things up right now." Then she turns toward the entrance, opens the door, and walks in. After I exchange a glance with Smile, we follow her lead.

Inside, we find Yasuyuki, or Toughboy, on the floor by the counter, packing records into a cardboard box and mumbling, "This sucks *so* hard," to himself. His cat—I think his name is Tom—is close by, resting on a pile of records and looking down at Toughboy like he is supervising him.

"Going well?" Tsubaki asks.

"I'm doing it. I'm doing it..." Toughboy sullenly stands up and turns toward us. "...Oh? What's up with you guys?"

He clearly wants to know why we are in here.

"Oh, just..."

"Just?" He raises an eyebrow at my vague reply.

The interior looks pretty much the same as before, tons of records still lining the racks and filling up the tables.

"Mr. Fujiyama..."

Smile quietly speaks up as she looks at the jackets on the racks. Everyone looks at her. She turns toward us.

"I think he wants to hear Sakura's voice." Her voice is full of conviction. "That's why he keeps looking around for it..."

Guess Smile reached the same conclusion I did. The article up at Mt. Umafuse. *Yamazakura*, the record Mr. Fujiyama's wife, Sakura, produced. Her singing voice would almost certainly be on that record. What he told us, through the tears: "*If I could hear it again...I could remember.*" Once he hears Sakura on the record, he'll remember...something.

Sakura petals, they fade on the wind without a word of farewell. That phrase is playing in my head again. The *Sakura* fade away—separation, and death.

I look around the store again. The store was established in order to sell

Sakura's records. He accumulated so many more. Mr. Fujiyama's memories… All these stacks and shelves seemed to me like Mr. Fujiyama's memories themselves. But the store's closing next week. Mr. Fujiyama's memories will disappear.

"Hey, um…"

I have to squeeze my voice out. The eyes staring at Smile earlier are now on me. Smile's are among them.

I look at a nearby table, picking up one of the cardboard boxes filled with records.

"…Is it all right if I help clean these up, too?"

The question is for Tsubaki, asked with all the power I can muster. She looks back at me in surprise.

"What?"

"Because I'm thinking the record Mr. Fujiyama's looking for might be in here somewhere."

And while we are packing everything up anyway, I want a chance to check on every record in the store. That is my request.

Tsubaki's expression turns serious—maybe a little angry, even. It scares me. But I want to do what I can here.

"Whoa, man…"

Toughboy, not understanding our intentions, tries to intervene.

"Wait! Me too!"

But Smile's perky voice cuts him off.

"Let me help you, too, please!"

The voice gives me courage.

Tsubaki is still staring at our copy of the article. She said she has no memory of her mother at all, right? Part of me wonders what Tsubaki thinks of this—seeing her young mother in the photo, even younger than Tsubaki is now.

"…I was actually looking for it, too."

I didn't expect that. After Mr. Fujiyama fell ill, Smile brought up the record to Tsubaki and she didn't react at all. But she is interested after all?

"After we decided to shut the store down, Dad suddenly started tearing up the racks and stuff. I always cleaned up afterward, but…" Now she is baring the Fujiyama family's secrets to me. I feel like I'm trespassing on something I wasn't supposed to see or hear about. It makes my heart ache.

"He kept saying he was looking for Sakura's record. I helped him look, but we didn't really know what it looked like, even."

I can imagine what kind of needle in the haystack it is.

"It was so tiring," she says softly, looking around the store. "But this record in Mom's left hand… It has to be the one Dad's looking for."

"I think so, yes."

Tsubaki falls silent. Quiet reigns in the store. Even Toughboy, perhaps sensing his mother's serious mood, keeps quiet.

After a few moments of silence, Tsubaki slowly looks up and smiles.

"…You think we'll find it if we all look?"

Her voice is so soft…but I can sense the will behind it. I am glad for that—more than anything, for the fact that Tsubaki understands my inspiration. Smile must have felt the same way because now she is next to me, nodding energetically. Even through the mask, I can tell she has a big smile on her face. It makes me feel even more optimistic.

"Let's get Beaver and Japan to help us, too."

"Sure!"

"Whoa, whoa, wait a second!"

Toughboy—left by the side of the road in this conversation—must be getting frustrated. Tom climbs onto his shoulder, looking at us like he is demanding an explanation.

"I know you're all excited and stuff, but what *is* this record Grandpa's looking for?!"

"You want to hear it, too, don't you?" Tsubaki says to Toughboy as she shows him the article. "It's Grandma's voice."

Wednesday, August 14

"You're not making much progress packing, Yui…"

Mom is looking around my room.

"You started so early, too. We move this weekend, you know?"

"I know, Mom…"

I sling my fanny pack around my shoulder, take my phone off my desk, and leave the room.

"I'm gonna be back a little late today."

"All right. Oh, you forgot your headphones!"

"I'm good, Mom."

Smile is already at Mr. Fujiyama's store when I arrive. She has a mask on again, but this time, she has her hair in a ponytail, which makes me avert my eyes shyly. She's just as cute that way, too.

Beaver and Japan join us, and so the six of us, including Toughboy and Tsubaki, begin our record hunt. Toughboy keeps chasing Beaver around, which doesn't help us much, but he reluctantly stops after Tsubaki yells at him.

We have a pretty simple procedure going. One by one, we open up each record jacket and check what is inside. First, we check to see if there is a duplicate of the jacket Mr. Fujiyama cherished so much. We don't stop there, though; we check the contents of each one as well. Maybe Sakura's record got mixed up with some other jacket. The contents are what matter, and our mission is to find the picture disc mentioned in that article, the one with Sakura's smiling face on it. If both an album and its contents aren't the one we are looking for, off it goes into a cardboard box for the junk haulers. Anything we discover, we share with the rest of the group.

Our deadline is the sixteenth—Friday, the day after tomorrow. That's when the collectors are coming. We need to finish the search and clean things up before then.

…In other words, the day before my family moves out. No matter how you slice it, I have zero time to work with.

"It's *so* hot…"

Smile stops sifting through records for a moment to fan her face.

"Yeah…"

"I'm melting over here."

Japan and Beaver both agree.

"What do you want?" Toughboy is dripping with sweat himself. "The AC's busted. You should be glad we at least got a fan."

The evening's one thing, but it's way too hard to go without air-conditioning in the middle of a day this insanely hot. The only fan they provided is the little one on top of the refrigerator, and we aren't getting any air from it because Tom is sitting right in front of it, tail tucked between his legs.

But even under these grueling conditions, Smile is masked up. She'll occasionally stop working to pull her mask out a bit and try to fan some air into the gap, but otherwise it stays on. She must be dying.

"…Why don't you take that off?"

"Huh?!"

She sounds more shocked than I expected.

"N-no, uh, look at all the dust!"

Clearly, the idea upsets her. Maybe I shouldn't have made the suggestion. Sorry, I guess?

"All right," Tsubaki finally says, "how about we break for lunch? Are cold *soumen* noodles okay with all of you?"

The living room of Mr. Fujiyama's house is shaded and much more comfortable. The *soumen* noodles we eat at the round table on the tatami mats are chilled, tasty, and couldn't have hit the spot any more.

"Hey," Japan says, refraining from stuffing himself for a moment, "where did Smile go?"

She isn't in the living room.

"She said something about being on a diet…"

That's exactly what Smile told me earlier: "I'll keep looking at the records, so you guys go ahead."

"A diet? She's already thin enough…"

Japan looks both impressed and distressed, but then he goes right back to his bowl of noodles. Toughboy and Beaver don't seem to care much about her because they are happily slurping away during this whole conversation.

Wrapping up lunch early, I go back to the store by myself. Smile is nowhere to be found there, either. I look outside and hear the sound of water dripping on the ground from a small passageway next to the building. There is a garden faucet there, and the water that comes out is flowing straight into Smile's mask-less mouth.

Nimbly hiding behind the building so she doesn't see me, I peek my head out for another look. Smile is drinking water like her life depends on it, her mouth and throat moving a little with each swallow. I can see droplets of water soaking into the mask on her chin. Her clear white teeth run back and forth over the spigot.

I can't take my eyes off her. I want to keep looking. I know I'm not supposed to, and I don't want her to see me...but I can't stop myself from watching.

"Phewww..."

With a sigh, Smile stands up. I reflexively hide myself.

"Ugh, I feel reborn..."

The sound of water hitting the ground disappears. I look again and see Smile wiping her mouth, a look of satisfaction on her face. Then I hear a loud growl from her stomach, loud enough that I can hear it over where I am. She puts a hand to her stomach, looking a bit distressed. Water alone probably won't be enough—the "diet" story is probably a lie, too. She has to take off her mask to eat, and while around other people, she doesn't want to.

So I leave the scene, not wanting to reveal I was watching her, and go back to the store. Japan and the rest have just wrapped up their noodle lunch. It is time to start sifting again.

The search continues until evening, and by then we've made it through about half the inventory. Sakura's record isn't there.

"Nothing so far," mutters Smile.

"We still have half of them left," I say. I want to remind Smile—and myself, too—not to give up hope.

I am back home that night. First I spend all day working through Mr. Fujiyama's pile of records, and now I'm working through my own belongings here... It gives me a sense of déjà vu, kind of.

It is time to pack for my impending move. Once again, I marvel at how many books I own. It almost looks like Mr. Fujiyama's record shop in here. Most of the books are related to haiku, including more back issues of *Haiku Monthly* than I remembered. No matter how many I put into boxes, more just seem to pop up everywhere.

When I finally finish packing the pile from the shelves next to my desk, I stop. Suddenly, reality hits me.

In a short while, I won't be able to see Smile. If I keep preparing for this move, I won't see her anymore. If we find Mr. Fujiyama's record, I won't be able to search for it with Smile. I feel kind of…off. What's up with this feeling? I hate it. It's all muddled… Seriously, what is this?

Wanting to take my mind off things, I put my hand on a shelving box and lift it up. I am about to leave the room and take it to my father's study, but then I hear a rustling sound and stop. Turning around, I see a magazine lying beside the desk—another issue of *Haiku Monthly*. There it is again. Somehow it has fallen between the desk and the shelf, and I never noticed.

I put the box on the floor and pick up the copy of *Haiku Monthly*.

"…Ah."

Looking at the cover makes me gasp a bit.

Special Feature: Introducing the Seasonal Words of Spring

The True Meaning of Seasonal Words (Spring)— ### Kotobuki Yamaji

+ Exploring the truth behind terms like *spring moon, thin ice, sowing seeds, white fish, mountain blossoms,* etc.
+ Differentiating Between Similar Seasonal Words (Emi Chiba)
+ Review: Danchidan (Furan Konii), Kadokawa Haiku Collection
+ Practical Tips: Expressing Separation

Mountain blossoms. A seasonal term for spring…

The next thing I know, I am sitting in my desk chair with the issue open on the table.

* * *

It is a March issue of *Haiku Monthly* from around ten years ago; I think I borrowed it from Dad way back when. He is the one who told me about *Haiku Monthly* first; it's been published ever since he was a student, so it goes way back. Now that I'm a haiku addict myself, I never miss an issue.

The section about mountain blossoms is near the middle of the magazine, in a sidebar titled "Haiku Meanderings."

Haiku Meanderings

In ancient folklore, a person with buckteeth was called a "mountain blossom," purportedly because its leaves appear before its blossoms. The earliest examples of this term date from the late nineteenth century, but the play on words may go as far back as the Edo period of the seventeenth century. A similar example is the *higan* cherry blossom, which blooms without leaves and is thus called *ubazakura* (old woman cherry blossom) because of its "toothless" appearance. Bashō used this expression to compose the poem, *"Happy memories formed by a wizened cherry in its final bloom."*

"People with buckteeth were called mountain blossoms?"

As I read it out loud, I can clearly picture Smile drinking water from that faucet earlier today. The way her mouth and throat rhythmically moved as she drank. Her mask getting damp. Her white buckteeth, moving amid the flow.

...I've got it. I have an idea. My face is burning. My fingertips feel weirdly sensitive, as if just touching this magazine is building a connection to my brain. My heart stirs; my emotions spill over. Then the words. I can't hold back my feelings for Smile.

...I've got haiku. I can always use words to express my feelings.

Placing *Haiku Monthly* on my desk, I pick up my phone, driven by my feelings. I have to write this now. I quickly tap the Curiosity icon and post my feelings as each one comes to mind.

Cherry @ Haiku account

Leaves hidden among
the boundless mountain blossoms

I love you so much
#haiku

I wait until it's time to go to bed, but Smile never gives it a like.

Words exist so that we can all convey the roar within each of us

Thursday, August 15

Another sweltering day. Under my mask it's like a sauna. I'm sweating so much, I'm afraid my sunscreen is dripping off.

I just realized that summer vacation will be over in about two weeks. Just like that... Tomorrow some guys will come to Mr. Fujiyama's store and take all his records, so we have to finish cleaning up today and find the one we need. I know that well enough...but my hands just won't reach out for the pile of records in front of me. I just keep staring at the mountain of vinyl; I can't lift my head.

I can't stop thinking about the haiku Cherry posted yesterday.

"I wonder what Sakura thought about hers..."

Last night, I was lying on my back in bed, looking at my phone. Julie and Marie were both asleep. The room was dark, the screen of my phone the only illumination. On the screen was a picture of that old newspaper article. Sakura was holding the record jacket in her right hand and a disc with her face on it in her left, smiling cheerfully.

That smile's just *so* cute.

I put my index finger and thumb around Sakura's face, expanding and pinching. Sakura's mouth filled the screen. *You've got buckteeth, Sakura. Just like me.*

She was smiling with her mouth wide open, which made them stand out a ton. But Sakura's smile was still bright and cheerful, like she didn't care about them at all. If she was embarrassed about it or didn't want people to see her smile, there's no way she'd be able to grin wide like that. *I* sure couldn't.

It's kind of blinding…

I was going to close the photo app and go straight to bed, but I thought I'd browse Curiosity real quick first. Checking my timeline just before bed's become a tough habit to break. Curiosity's more lively at night. I guess a lot of people are like me, posting and commenting just before they hit the sack.

Then a familiar headphone icon appeared on my timeline.

`Cherry @ Haiku account`

`Leaves hidden among`
`the boundless mountain blossoms`
`I love you so much`
`#haiku`

Oh, a haiku from Cherry. A new one…

"Leaves hidden among the boundless mountain blossoms…"

I said it out loud. Then suddenly, my mouth stopped moving. Not because I didn't want to keep reading it. In fact, I really wanted to.

"…I love you so much."

Saying that made me feel like my heart would stop. Why? I didn't even know why. It was so strange, like my whisper was bouncing off my phone screen and throwing itself right back into my face. When I said it out loud—when I made the sound—it was just, like…so direct. It's just words, but I can still vividly picture Cherry's face turning red like a cherry. I was beside myself. My heart beat so fast. It's painful…but somehow, so happy, too. Why?

In my head, Cherry, with his bright red face, was saying, "I love you so much," out loud. I love you…so much.

Sometimes I get comments like that when I stream on Curiolive. *I love you, Smile!* and so on. It's not that I dislike that. Being loved makes me feel accepted, and that's always a nice thing. But it doesn't make me *this* tense.

"*Leaves* hidden." Is he sure that's what he meant? He didn't mean to write *teeth* in there and autocorrect messed up for him, or something? …I'm over-thinking this way too much. But it seemed so obvious. Teeth…hidden among the blossoms. *Did you see them, Cherry?*

So many feelings swirled around in my heart. Up and down, over and over. What was this? Why? My body hadn't moved a muscle for several minutes. I *couldn't* move. I was just looking at Cherry's haiku on my phone, but my mind was running as fast as it could. Why?

Something appeared in front of my phone, blocking my vision. My mind was moving so fast that I didn't realize until later that it was my own right hand. My finger went to the "♡" mark right below Cherry's haiku. *Let's like it per usual…* But no, I couldn't do what I normally did. I got so close to the "♡" mark, and then my hand stopped. I wanted to like it… I couldn't press it. I wanted to. *Let's do it. Push the like button…*

Suddenly, the light disappeared. The screen showing Cherry's haiku just a moment ago lost its backlight. Instead, all I saw was my face. I didn't need to turn on a light to see how red I was. It made them stick out even more. I didn't want to see that—those big white teeth. The braces… It's *gross*.

My right hand—about to press the LIKE button—went up to my mouth as if sucked in. I touched my teeth. They felt vaguely warm. The image of me on the screen wasn't cute at all. I hated it. I didn't want to look at it. I didn't want to be seen. Seen by whom? …By Cherry.

I felt a *pop!* like something blew up. The next thing I knew, I was slamming my phone case shut as hard as I could.

I pick up a record from the pile. It has a white background with a brown-tinted print of an old man and woman, like something out of a woodcut. *SONGS* is written on the bottom; that must be the title.

But I am really just pretending to think about the jacket in front of me. My antenna is pointed right at Cherry, diagonally across from me to the left, where the fan noise is coming from. My eyes have been locked on this old couple on the jacket for a while now, but they seem out of focus…or really, all my nerves feel like they are on the left side of my body. I don't know if it's the heat of the room or the mask I'm wearing, or the continual pounding of my heart since yesterday, but it's hot. My face is just so hot.

I check inside the jacket. It is a normal black record. Lifting my sullen face, I put *SONGS* in the "to trash" cardboard box and shift my eyes toward Cherry. Natural. Totally natural.

Cherry is silently working away, just as he did yesterday… Sweat is beading on his cheeks. It falls on the records, splashing. He doesn't seem to notice.

…Ah!

I involuntarily look away… Our eyes had met. My body hasn't moved at all until a moment ago, but now I suddenly turn on and start rummaging through the pile. Take a jacket, check inside, stick it in a box, take a jacket, check inside, stick it in a box…

Evening comes all too quickly.

We've all worked hard to whittle down the pile, and now Cherry is holding the last album. We have checked every other album and jacket, but we never did find Sakura's smile.

So we put the boxes out on the porch or the courtyard, along with the speakers and other stuff inside the store. The place is now just racks, tables, a refrigerator, and a fan. Without the records, there is suddenly a lot of empty space.

Everyone gathers around Cherry, focusing on that last record. I feel like I am praying a bit, too. *Come on out, Sakura.*

Slowly, Cherry holds up the jacket in front of him. I gently put my right hand inside and grab the record. Pulling it out…

It is a black disc. Cherry slowly turns it over. Still pitch-black. Sakura's smile isn't there.

"Damn, so it wasn't here after all?" spits out Toughboy before storming out the back door. Japan and Beaver follow soon after.

"Well," Tsubaki says in her kind voice, "thank you." Looking up, I see her with her hand on Cherry's shoulder, smiling warmly. Cherry keeps his head down, not answering.

"You too, Smile."

Tsubaki looks at me and smiles. I can't speak, so all I can do is give her a small shake of my head. We got her so fired up that she searched for this record alongside us, but we came up with nothing. It feels like we are just rubbing salt in her old wounds. I feel terrible about it, and I think Cherry does, too. It's so frustrating. Cherry looks like he's overflowing with all kinds of emotions.

Slowly, he looks up. He scans the store, as if refusing to give up, as if he is still searching for something in a completely record-less store.

"Yasuyuki! Can you carry the fridge and the fan out?"

Tsubaki walks out the back door, Tom in her arms.

"Huhhh?! Ohhh, all *riiight*..."

"Thank you."

We can hear her and Toughboy talking outside.

The next thing I know, Cherry—seated next to me just now—has moved in front of the refrigerator Tom had been sitting on. He crouches down, staring right at it. What's gotten into him?

I approach him from behind. It is a pretty old fridge, very different from the one at my place. It only goes up to around chest height, for one, with one small door up top and a bigger one on the bottom. The pull handles are on one side of the unit; the one back home opens out from the middle. The fan on top of it (which Tom was hogging earlier) has been turned off—by Tsubaki, I suppose—after staying on for nearly two days straight.

Cherry grabs the top handle of the refrigerator and slowly opens it. It is dark inside, like it isn't turned on, and there is nothing in it. Not just food or ice or whatever—there aren't even any shelves or anything. Then Cherry opens the bottom door. Nothing. There is a crisper tray and a rack for eggs and stuff, but nothing else.

Hanging his head a bit, Cherry stands up and closes both doors. There is a wet slamming sound that kind of sticks in our ears.

"Dammit..."

I think he was actually looking to see if there were records in the fridge. His last hope, kind of. But it's empty.

"...In between."

What? In between? What's he mean? Suddenly, Cherry stretches out. I take a step backward, surprised.

The refrigerator is positioned so it is adjacent to the counter by the wall, next to the back door. Cherry peers into the gap, then grabs the refrigerator with both hands and begins to shift it away from the wall. The refrigerator slowly moves away, making a scratching sound.

Once it is a few inches apart, the area behind it is revealed. It must've been hidden for a long time because the green paint on the wall is discolored in a neat rectangle the exact shape of the fridge. It looks brand-new, in fact. There is a little dust at the foot of it.

And a pink, square shape is mixed in with the white dust. It has a round hole in the middle, a big smile peeking out. Then, in perfect sync, Cherry and I shout:

"There it is!"

The store looks pretty lonely without any records in it, but I am as chipper as could be. I think everyone else is, too. Smiles for miles. I'm so glad to see Mr. Fujiyama look as happy as he does.

Sakura's record was in the store the whole time. Cherry didn't give up until the bitter end, and I think Sakura rewarded that.

When Tsubaki went off to tell Mr. Fujiyama that we found it, the news seemed to improve his health immediately. Now he is sitting on a chair in front of me, looking elated as he stares at the record with Sakura's smile printed on it.

He has two jackets now, the one we found and the empty one he always carries around, and there is one in each of his hands. We had been looking for the record inside the empty one, but we never did find it. Lucky thing, I think, that he happened to have a duplicate. Tsubaki *did* mention that he started this store in order to sell her records, and I'm sure he must've had more than one of Sakura's in stock. Guess this one literally fell between the cracks.

To be honest, though, I still have a question or two. For one, where did the record that goes with Mr. Fujiyama's empty jacket go? Maybe it's somewhere in the mall still.

"Sakura," Mr. Fujiyama mumbles in a wobbly voice. Tears are trickling down his cheeks—completely different from the sad tears he'd cried the other day. These come from a place of joy. I almost cry, too, as I watch. He is certainly satisfied enough with this, and I'm sure the record's identical anyway. Now he'll finally get to listen to the voice he sought for so long.

"I'll have Japan play it for you, okay?"

I take the newfound jacket from Mr. Fujiyama. The store had some turntables set up, but we had put them away with the boxes of records. "I'll get everything set up for it right away!" Japan exclaims, which is awfully nice of him.

After a few moments: "Hey, where are the speaker cords?" Japan looks up from the racks of record players and other machines. "The speakers won't work without them."

"Oh, I think I saw some on the porch."

Cherry jogs out the back door. While we wait for him, I take the record out of the jacket, figuring I'd keep things moving along. Sakura's smile is right there, printed on the record, just as shown in the newspaper article. It's *so* cute. But what's on the other side of it? ...Oh. Fireworks.

Side B has a photograph of a bunch of fireworks shooting up from a rice paddy, all beautiful and colorful. I immediately recognize it as a scene from the Daruma Festival. This record has to be decades old, but the photo hasn't faded at all. It is just as cute as Sakura herself, even.

So they could print two different pictures on each side of a record? These picture discs are pretty neat, actually.

...I'd love to show Cherry.

And then my feelings, overflowing from the glass of my soul in an instant, brings me right out the back door.

Cherry is just turning around toward the house when I step onto the porch. He has a rolled-up cord in his hand; I can tell he's found what he wanted.

"Hey, look!"

I run up to him, holding the record in front of my chest, stretching my arms way out so he can see all the fireworks.

"...Fireworks?"

Cherry looks at me.

"Isn't it cute?"

"Cute...?"

"Yeah!" I turn the record over and look at it again. The bright fireworks are dazzling, as if the light is shining on my face. Incredibly cute. Today's the fifteenth, so this year's Daruma Festival is two days away, on the seventeenth.

"The festival's the day after tomorrow, isn't it...?"

...I feel hot. My face and head are so hot. Why? Because I want...to see the fireworks. With Cherry.

"Do you...?"

I want to see them with him. I want to. I want to... But it's so embarrassing. I can't look at Cherry... I want to. I want to see them with him.

"Do you want to watch the fireworks...with me?"

The mask rubs against my face. My voice is so soft, I am sure only I can hear it. My gaze drifts off toward the loop of electrical cord twisted in Cherry's hand. His fingers are wiggling around, putting kinks in it.

"Um..."

Cherry speaks. My eyes shoot up to his face. He has his head lowered, face blushing red. Once I know our eyes won't be meeting, it is easy for me to keep staring at his face.

...Wait. This reaction. It means he fully understands what I just said. It's a date. I asked him out on a date. And then Cherry goes bright red, and... Oh, man, so *that's* how it is? No way. Really?

"Cherry!"

Suddenly, a loud voice comes from the back door.

"Get the cord over here already!"

It's Japan's voice. I turn around to find him peeking out from behind the rack, urging us back inside.

"Oh," Cherry murmurs. It feels like the air has been taken out of the porch. The atmosphere is just so...

I look down at the floor, unable to say anything. I can see Cherry's feet.

His sneakers begin moving slowly toward the back door. I just follow them with my eyes.

"…Okay!"

Cherry's voice—that booming "*Okay!*"—fades away with his footsteps. It keeps on echoing in my ears, though.

He said okay. I'm going to watch the fireworks with him.

Goose bumps. My mind floods. From the tips of my toes to the top of my head, sheer joy runs through my body at incredible speed.

…I did it. I did it. I did it! Yes! Yessss!!

I hold the record tightly in both hands. My body jumps up and down on its own. I can't stop. I'm so happy, I can't. It's the happiest I've ever been in my life. I've never been this happy. It's not an exaggeration. I'm so happy, I feel like I'm going to faint.

…Yes. Yes! Yesss!!

I never knew I could ever actually feel like this. I can't help it if I didn't, though. Like, it's the first time. For the first time, I know now. This is love.

I'm in love with Cherry.

And once I realize it for myself, it makes me feel a bit calmer, weirdly. The joy was storming through me like a train earlier, but now it feels more like it's slowly seeping in, giving my body time to absorb it. I'm just *so* happy.

I carefully relax my grip on the record I am hugging, then take another look at Side B. I'll get to see these fireworks with Cherry. It's a date. That's so wonderful…

…Oh?

After I calm down a bit, I feel something strange about the record in my hand. From the side, it looks kind of wavy—and come to think of it, the surface feels a bit warped in my hands, too. That is much clearer to see when I place it atop a tatami mat on the porch. There are a ton of gaps between the record and the mat. It is definitely warped.

"Wow, will this even work?"

Maybe it's because I hugged it too hard just now? It'll sound a lot better if it's flat, I assume. So I put some weight on it, pushing it down on the tatami mat in an attempt to flatten it out with my hands. I'm not really thinking. I just don't realize that records can break so easily.

The moment I place my weight on it, a sharp cracking sound echoes across the courtyard, which is growing cooler now that it's evening. It is so sharp, it feels like the cracks extend deep into my hands. The blood drains from my face, my feet, everywhere at once. Suddenly, my body feels cold, the moisture in my mask clammy.

I slowly lift my hands. Some pieces of vinyl stick to my hand for a moment before gravity audibly peels them off.

"Oh no…"

The part of the record I'd put my hands on, there atop the tatami mat, is now shattered into fragments.

"Smile?"

I turn around at the sound of Cherry's voice, startled so much that my heart nearly jumps out of my chest.

Crack!

The sound is even sharper than before. Slowly, I begin to realize that things are only getting worse. I was so startled by Cherry calling for me that I turned around, arms over the record to hide it, only to lose my balance and fall right back on the tatami mat, butt first.

"Hey… What's up?"

My eyes have been locked with his for a few moments now. He was casually asking at first, but now I think he can tell something is wrong. The tone of his voice grew darker.

Slowly, I raise my arms up from behind my back and let them fall slack. I hate to look, but I have to. I know I have to, but my body won't listen to me. But I *have* to…

I twist my upper body around, creakily, like the handlebars of a rusted bicycle—so hard that I think I can hear the creaking. On the tatami, Sakura's smile is scattered around, the fragments sharply pointed like glass.

Friday, August 16

My eyes are red as an albino rabbit's. Red around the eyes, too. Looking in the mirror, I can tell I'm a mess in all kinds of ways.

After that whole ordeal, I was so distraught that I could barely keep hold of myself. Tsubaki kept consoling me, telling me not to worry about it. I apologized over and over to Mr. Fujiyama, but I was crying so hard, not even I was sure of exactly what I was saying. What I do remember, though, is that I was just too scared to look Mr. Fujiyama in the eye.

They kept consoling me for a while until I finally calmed down a bit, and Cherry walked me home. Even back there, I was crying way too much to sleep at all. Mom, Dad, Julie, and Marie all tried to make me feel better. *Everybody* was feeling sympathetic toward me last night. But whenever I pictured Mr. Fujiyama's face, the tears rolled right back out again. I spent the whole night curled up in bed.

"Did you lose your phone again?" Marie asked, but really, I'd take losing my phone over *this* any day. The record was all warped, so I thought I needed to fix it. But I shouldn't have done anything. I made a mistake I can never take back. It was Mr. Fujiyama's most precious memory, and I destroyed it.

I look at the clock. It's getting close to noon. My work shift at Sunnyside begins at one today, but to be honest, I'm afraid to go. But I have to. I have to apologize to Mr. Fujiyama one more time.

So I report to Sunnyside, but Mr. Fujiyama isn't there. A message is scribbled on the whiteboard reading, *Fujiyama off today*, which depresses me even further.

Nobody else at Sunnyside—neither Nami, her coworkers, nor the day's group of clients—has heard about the record yet, it seems. They are all as cheerful as usual, saying hello to me like they always do, but they can tell right away that I'm depressed. "What's wrong?" they all ask, worried about me, but I can't tell them about the record. I guess they understand that because nobody pries too much...

...Cherry included. He doesn't say anything, and I am too embarrassed to speak up. I don't even thank him for taking me home yesterday. Even during our Daruma Ondo dance rehearsal, we seem distant from each other, somehow. Time seems to slow to a crawl.

"Okay, everyone, the show begins on the roof at seven PM tomorrow!"
"Don't forget your yukata!"

It's just before five in the afternoon when Nami and Akiko give us that final reminder. My shift for today is almost over, and so is Cherry's.

"Cherry?"

I call out to him as he is cleaning up. He jerks up a bit, startled, and turns around. I turn my head, avoiding eye contact, but as I do, I see he is wearing his headphones around his neck.

"Um…" I have to work hard to squeeze my voice out. "Can you…join me after this? I want to…like, really apologize to Mr. Fujiyama one more time…"

"Oh… Sure. Of course…"

Cherry's voice is as soft as mine.

"Thanks…"

I need to thank Cherry for yesterday. I have to apologize for breaking the record… I have to say all of that. But…I can't find my voice. I'm afraid if I put my feelings into words, I'll be admitting that the events of yesterday really did happen. It's scary. And yeah, they *did* happen, but I'm scared to admit it. That is the feeling that fills my heart right now.

"Um…"

I hear Cherry's mumbled voice through the invisible barrier of air between him and me. I look up a little, bringing my gaze up to around his midsection. Just like me, he is wearing a name tag written for him by Nami. The word *Cherry* wavers in the air. Cherry himself is silent, but *Cherry* on his tag keeps on wobbling around.

"Actually, I wanted to—"

"Hello!"

An unfamiliar, cheerful voice drowns out Cherry's. It comes from the entrance.

From where I am in the staff space, I can see the woman from the other side of the partition. Cherry, his back to the entrance, turns around and looks at her.

"Oh! Maria! It's been forever!"

Nami approaches the woman, a cheerful smile on her face.

"Hi," the woman says, waving. Akiko and our senior clients gather around her, everyone chatting with a smile on their face.

"How's your back? Feeling better now?" Ms. Tanaka gets up from her desk and walks right past me and Cherry to see the visitor.

The woman rubs her lower back. "Yes, thank you," she says with a smile. Everyone at Sunnyside is in front of the entrance now, except for me and Cherry.

"Cherry did a great job subbing in for you, Maria."

"Oh, yes! He was such a great help!"

Nami and Akiko are all smiles. "Was he?" Maria replies with a grin. "That's good. I was a little worried…"

It seems like everyone knows her…but Cherry was subbing for her?

"…Who is she?"

I look at Cherry. He is slumped over, a pained look on his face. He blinks a few times, then he forces the words out.

"…My mom."

What do you mean? Your mother? She's replacing you? No, no. Cherry is subbing for her… Wait, what? Why?

"Thanks," Maria says as she bows, "for treating my son so well." Everyone around her bows politely in response.

"Not at all. And thanks for all of your hard work up to now, Mrs. Sakura." Ms. Tanaka looks back at Cherry and slowly bows.

"Yeah, great job!" chimes in Nami.

"I wish," Akiko adds, "we could've done the Daruma Ondo dance together tomorrow…"

"Sorry about that! My husband's job, you know… And sorry to you, too, Yui."

Nami, Akiko, Maria… They are all talking to Cherry, even his own mother, and he keeps staring silently at the floor.

And all I can do is stare at him.

The frogs' croaking in the rice paddies seems louder than ever before to me that evening… Or maybe not. It's more because Cherry and I have remained totally silent this whole time.

The ruts slowly drift behind us. Mixed in with the frogs, I can hear our footsteps—*trudge, trudge, trudge*. A very slow tempo.

"…I'm sorry I didn't tell you about…the move."

"…When did you know?"

"…When…summer break started."

"…What about the fireworks?"

Our footsteps stop at the same time.

The frogs. The rice plants swaying around, scraping against one another. The irrigation canal. The cars on the main road. The wind.

Then my voice, lost in the mask. "I asked…if we could watch them together…"

"…I'm sorry."

Cherry's voice is the quietest I have ever heard it, but it reaches me. For some reason, I remember the sound of the record shattering, the feel of the shards peeling off my hand.

"…Oh."

My cheeks hurt from the mask rubbing against them as I speak. My ears hurt, too. The braces are clamped down on my front teeth, making them ache.

It hurts. Everything hurts. It hurts to be without him. I want to be with him. I just want to be with him. That's all.

"Well…good luck."

Trudge, trudge, trudge. My pace increases. His, I can't even hear. There is the sound of croaking… No, of crying. He's crying, and the sound is growing softer and softer.

It hurts. It hurts to be without him. I want that to stop.

I'm not sure how I make it there. The next thing I know, I am walking down the street where Mr. Fujiyama's record store is. The streetlights come and go, my shadow swinging back and forth with them. It is so painful to say goodbye to Cherry, I almost can't think about anything else—but I know I have to apologize to Mr. Fujiyama.

* * *

There is a small figure in front of the store. It is too dark to tell who it is at first, but as I slowly approach, I recognize the cotton-ball hair of Mr. Fujiyama. He is a little ways in front of the store, looking upward. I follow his gaze and see that he is looking at the roof. That's where I looked, too, the first time I came here. There used to be that sign, the mountain with FUJIYAMA RECORDS written on it, but now there's nothing. It makes me stop in my tracks. Of course, it'd be gone. They shut down the store.

I look at Mr. Fujiyama again. The way he is quietly staring where the sign used to be... He must be in a lot of pain. I really did something terrible to him. My chest hurts. The record, saying good-bye to Cherry... It all hurts. Sakura's smiling face, all broken and scattered across the tatami mat, flashes in my mind. The record is broken. If I could go back in time, I wouldn't have tried to bend it back in place, but I can't. I can't unbreak it. When things fall apart, all you can do is leave. Parting is the only way...even if you want to be with them. You've got to separate.

But I want to stay. I want to be with him. I want to—wait. Suddenly, I recall something. I don't know if it'll work out. But I want to give it a shot.

"Mr. Fujiyama?"

He slowly turns his head toward me.

"Can I borrow that record, please?"

I apologize to Mr. Fujiyama, then tell him about the idea I had. He smiles and lends me the broken record, along with the jacket. I take it home with me, taking great care not to lose a single fragment.

Now all the pieces are lined up on the desk in our common space. Next to them is superglue I borrowed from Dad. I will put all the pieces back together, reconstructing Sakura's smiling face, and then we can listen to it. That was my idea.

I want Mr. Fujiyama to hear Sakura's voice. That desire is still as strong as ever. But I also have this impossible hope that if I can restore this record, maybe that'll also mend my relationship with Cherry, somehow. I know it's an impossible hope. I know Cherry is moving away. But...

...For now, fixing the record comes first. It's the only thing I can do.

* * *

The pieces are scattered like broken glass, but the smallest one is only about the size of my pinkie. If I follow the shape like a puzzle, it is bound to become a perfect circle again—and in an added stroke of luck, the warping on the pieces makes it easier to identify which one goes where. Thanks to that, every piece is aligned correctly in just about an hour's time.

From there, I use superglue to reattach the pieces. Back when I was a kid, we did this stream once where we glued one of Dad's model kits back together after Marie broke it. Julie bawled her eyes out after getting the glue in her hair.

I pick up one of the pieces. I figured a record would be really thick because of how solid it is, but it's actually pretty thin—about as thin as a ruler. I have to be careful about how much glue I put on because otherwise some glue will ooze out and go all over the place. After applying the glue, I place the pieces next to one another, aligning their sides. Then I wait patiently. Even with superglue, you have to hold them in place for about twenty seconds—which shouldn't feel nearly as long as it does to me right now.

After a little while, I slowly remove one of my hands... Okay. They're attached! Now to put the rest of the record together! I have a lot of pieces, so I knew it'd be a challenge, but I am gonna have it done by tomorrow so Mr. Fujiyama can listen to it.

Now to apply glue to the next piece. Not too much...

Suddenly, my hand feels lighter. The piece I had glued on a minute ago falls off, bouncing a bit on the desk. Oh, great, it didn't harden all the way. I apply a second layer to this first piece, but the gunk from the first layer of glue keeps the two pieces from aligning evenly.

I am starting to get a bad feeling about this. I am trying to glue that first piece back on, but—ahhh, I knew it. That gunk is in the way. It's not lining up.

So now what? Try to pick off the crust with a hobby knife or a pair of scissors or something? But what if I damage the record more...? No, don't worry. Even if it's a little misaligned, I think it'll still be listenable. Let's keep going.

I continue putting the pieces together, this time giving the glue ample time to harden. It's night by now, so the room is quiet. I stare hard at the pieces. Time passes slowly.

Watching the pieces this intently, my mind begins to wander. His headphones on his head like a mohawk. Learning what a saijiki was. The first time we went home together, when I did all the talking. *Summer's lustrous sheen, there's a false start in the wind and the evening dusk.* "False start" was a cute way to put it. I look forward to him posting new haiku. It was fun adding my likes, too. Mt. Umafuse... Was that kind of like our first date? Mr. Fujiyama's record store was hot as an oven, wasn't it? Too bad we couldn't have those *soumen* noodles together. Kinda funny how we shouted out in unison when we found the record. I liked that. Guys have it easy when it comes to talking about themselves. When he wrote "*leaves*," was that...maybe autocorrect going haywire? Aren't these fireworks cute? Inviting him to see the fireworks with me...like, that was super embarrassing. And I heard him say it—say "*Okay!*" so clearly... Oh, wait. Or was he talking to Japan when he said that? That was the happiest moment of my life, too...and I had it all wrong... I have to try and fix this record. If I didn't screw up like that, Mr. Fujiyama would've heard Sakura's voice by now. But I just had to do that...

Slowly, I move one of my hands away. The pieces stay stuck together... at first. The fragment bounces off the desk again. I thought it was locked in place, but it fell again.

Tears fall on the pieces, bouncing off them. Several tears. I can't hold back. I can't stop the tears. I thought things were going to work out, but they didn't.

I've been doing nothing but crying since yesterday.

It hurts. My heart hurts so much.

I wake up. The room is bright.

Sitting up, I feel pain shoot up my back and elbows, like a rusty door. I turn around, look out the window, and realize the room is bathed in broad daylight. Past noon, maybe?

The clock on my desk says…a little before three. I'd fallen asleep at my desk.

"It's about time," Julie says, entering the room. "Here." She holds out a mug to me. I stare at it blankly, then accept it.

"Thanks," I say, taking a sip.

"It's tea. I left it at room temperature. Having an ice-cold drink right after waking up isn't good for you."

Julie smiles. She's so good to me. I take another sip of tea and put the mug on the desk. On the desk lay the fruits of last night's labor. A warped record, with all the pieces glued together. That cute smile of Sakura's is a bit marred by the glue splotches here and there, and it is slightly misaligned in spots. It's all in one piece, but it isn't exactly a perfect circle, and I really don't think it's playable. I don't know much about vinyl records, but I am pretty sure about that, at least.

"Hey…" Marie's cheerful voice echoes through the room. I look at the door and see half of her body leaning into the doorway, her finger beckoning me.

"Come on down to the living room."

I follow her downstairs. Julie joins us.

"Ah, you're finally up?" Dad smiles at me.

"Here, we got everything set up for you." Mom points to a flower-patterned yukata hanging off the rack—light pink, with a cute cherry blossom pattern. "I'll help you put it on, so get ready."

Ah, right. Today's the Daruma Festival. There are three sets of outfits, one each for me, Julie, and Marie.

"Cheer up, okay? Let's all go together."

Marie grabs my arm, smiling at me from down below.

"Yeah, I need a break from exam prep."

Julie is holding my other hand, smiling just as much.

Julie, Marie… I'm so glad to see you. And you too, Mom and Dad. My mind's in shambles, but everyone's so nice, and kind, and trying to cheer me up.

I can't really repair the record, but I'll give it back to Mr. Fujiyama anyway. That, and I'll apologize one more time. Julie and Marie are here for me right now, and that is a huge support for me.

Mom dresses me up and does my hair. I know I am in a fancy yukata and all, but I still don't want anyone to see my buckteeth, so I put on my mask, and the three of us leave the house.

"I'm really sorry."

I bow my head. It's the best apology I can give, and I hope it reaches him.

Looking up, I see Mr. Fujiyama staring at the patchwork record. Then he slowly looks me in the eye and nods, a kind smile on his face. Whew. That's great. He can understand how I feel. That smile really saves me.

"Oh, that's the record?" Nami comes closer, looking at the album in Mr. Fujiyama's hands.

"There's a photo on it?" Akiko asks, joining us.

"It's called a picture disc," I say.

"Ohhh…"

They both look impressed. I had told the staff about the record just now—how we all searched for it together and found it, only for me to shatter it.

Mr. Fujiyama hands the record to Nami. "Thank you," she says, accepting it with a smile. "This lady's cute, isn't she?"

"She's Mr. Fujiyama's wife, actually."

"She is?!"

Now they are even more intrigued. Nami turns the record over, revealing the fireworks photo—the fireworks from the Daruma Festival. My glue job didn't go all that well, so Side B looks a lot more misaligned, much to my chagrin.

Nami wrinkles her nose and holds the record close to her face.

"You know, I feel like I've seen this before…"

"Okay, everyone," Akiko says, turning around, "it's almost time for the performance. Ready to head up to the roof?"

That time already, huh? I look at the clock on the wall; it is just before six in the evening. We are set to perform at seven, doing the Daruma Ondo dance we spent so much time rehearsing up on the roof for the festival. She was right. It was about time to…head out…

…Huh. That's weird. I feel like I'm overlooking something really important.

"Once the factory closed down twenty-eight years ago, the Nouvelle company purchased both the land and the factory on it. Nouvelle builds and operates large-scale commercial sites across Japan, and they transformed the factory into a shopping mall, you see. When Nouvelle builds a large site like this, they make sure they don't completely erase the memory of what was there before, out of respect for the local community. Sometimes they use what was on-site for other purposes, or sometimes they use them to create a monument. I understand that over in the Kansai region, they built a mall over an old baseball stadium and kept the main grandstand intact inside it. In much the same way, this used to be a vinyl plant, so sometimes the clocks and other things you see around the mall are actually records."

Suddenly I recalled the story from the guide at the photo exhibition.

"Sometimes the clocks and other things you see around the mall are actually records."

"Ahhhh!!"

Nami's sudden shout interrupts my thought process, and it's so loud that I thought my heart would literally stop. She's pointing at something, a surprised look on her face. Following her finger, I see that she is pointing at the circular clock near the ceiling above the sofa where Mr. Fujiyama is sitting. It is the same clock I glanced at just now; it has been up at Sunnyside for as long as I've worked here. It's a picture of some fireworks and there are no numbers on it, which sometimes makes it hard to tell the time.

…Wait. This clock's fireworks… It's identical to Sakura's record.

I hurriedly take off my geta sandals and climb onto the sofa, taking the clock off the wall. Once it is safe in my hands, I give it a closer look.

"…Ah!"

Now I am shouting. Looking more closely, I notice there are tiny grooves on the surface, just like a record. I can identify that well enough after all the many records I handled and examined at Mr. Fujiyama's shop. This *has* to be a record.

The clock mechanism is on the other side of the hole, the long and short hands sticking out from it. The short hand just clicked in front of me—in front of that fireworks photo I thought was so cute.

With trembling hands, I flip it over. My eyes meet...with Sakura's! Carefully, I take the machine with batteries and stuff in the middle and slowly remove it. There, I find Sakura's smiling, unobstructed face.

"This is it! The record!"

I hurriedly hand it to Mr. Fujiyama. He greets it with total disbelief. "Sakura," he mumbles happily. How can I not believe in miracles now? This is totally amazing. I never expected to find Sakura's record right here in Sunnyside.

Nami sighs. "Wow, now I feel bad for Cherry. Talk about bad luck."

"Oh, I know," replies Akiko. "If he wasn't moving today, he'd be here to listen to this."

It's close to the evening now. Cherry's probably already left town...and we'll never listen to this together. I take my phone out of my handbag. My summer with Cherry began because I mistook his phone for mine. He looked hard for that record; he wanted Mr. Fujiyama to hear it, too. Now it is right here, but Cherry isn't. I sure wish I could hear Sakura's voice with him.

...The phone. Right, the phone. There's just one way left that we can listen to this record together, and this is it! And it'll require the help of everyone at Sunnyside—that, and Japan with his record expertise.

"Guys, I need all of your help!"

I shout loudly through my mask. This is the only thing I can do, and only I can do it.

Throughout my whole life, at last I find words bubble up like soda pop

The calendar is still hanging on the wall. Saturday, August 17.

Movers coming 4 PM.

I've seen that scribbled note many times by now. I wrote it myself, in fact. But now the day is here.

I remove the thumbtack holding the calendar to the wall. It leaves a small hole. I rub it a bit with my finger, but it doesn't go away. Ah well. It doesn't matter. I'm leaving anyway.

Now the packing process for the move is all done. I wrapped up everything after I left Smile yesterday. The packing was finished before I knew it; it was hard to believe I couldn't get it done before then. I fold the calendar in my hand twice, then toss it into the trash. I can hear the plastic liner rustle a little against the floor. I can always buy a new one.

Slowly, I look around the room. The evening sun is shining through the balcony, stopping right at my feet. It isn't a big room, but when it's empty like this, it sure feels spacious. I've been living in this complex for as long as I can remember, but now this barren room feels like it belongs to someone else. It's sweltering and humid because I just turned off the air conditioner. The sweat is making it feel like the headphones around my neck are sticking to my skin. I grab them with both hands and gently put them over my ears.

"Oh…"

Smile's voice is echoing in my head. The headphones' noise canceling only makes it clearer.

"Well…good luck."

The refrain of our separation booms in my brain. She didn't say good-bye. She didn't, which makes the sense of separation even stronger. Even though moving shouldn't make much of a difference, given our phones and all. The more I fell in love with Smile, the more difficult it was to tell her about the move.

…It wasn't that I couldn't. I just didn't want to. If I put it into words, that would make it come true. What was the point of that? It's not like that'd undo the move.

"Do you want to see the fireworks…with me?"

I've known I was moving out on the day of the Daruma Festival, but I still wanted to see the fireworks with Smile…but in the end, I couldn't give her more than some halfhearted pleasantries. I hurt her. It came out the wrong way to her… Or not? I really did want to join her. If I could have told her about the move earlier, maybe it wouldn't have worked out that way? …But now I'm just thinking about things that'll never happen. It's a waste of time.

…Then I hear the intercom from the hallway.

"Hello?"

Mom answers it from the dining room. The movers are here.

I take my phone out of my pocket and check the time. They were supposed to come at four, but the time is 5:23 PM. I guess they are a little late, but that's fine. We aren't due at the new place until tomorrow afternoon anyway. So I close my phone case and tuck it into my pocket.

The sunlight that used to be at my feet is now barely covering the toes on my left foot. I pull my left leg back and walk out of the room, that haiku dancing in my mind.

"Sakura petals, they fade on the wind without a word of farewell."

By the time we finish loading the moving truck, it is already dark.

The truck speeds off, and Dad follows it in our car, Mom in the passenger seat and me alone in the back.

* * *

The scenery passes by listlessly outside the window, one view giving way to the next without any input from me. The people on the sidewalks of the main road are dressed in yukata and *jinbei* short jackets, smiling and walking excitedly, having all kinds of fun. They are heading for the mall…to join the Daruma Festival.

My heart beats normally, thanks to my headphones. I'm not hearing any of the excitement from everyone going to the mall. The view passes me by. It's just normal scenery.

Ba-ding…

Suddenly, my headphones come to life, startling me. It's a notification, and it rudely pulls me back to reality. My field of vision narrows, my attention turning to the phone in my pocket.

I sit up a little and take out my phone. Opening the case, I press the side button. The screen lights up brightly in the dark car, the words jumping into view.

[Curiolive]
Smile has begun streaming.

I have no words. It's too surprising.

Smile has begun streaming? The time on my phone is 7:24. They should be dancing the Daruma Ondo right now. My heart is racing. Like I'm running the 100-meter dash… Hurry, hurry!

Quickly, I swipe the notification bar to launch Curiolive. The familiar user interface appears on the screen, showing a two-story festival tower decorated with red and white ribbons and lanterns, a crowd of spectators surrounding it. The sky is dark, but everything around the tower is brightly lit by the lanterns and food stalls. She is streaming live from the Daruma Festival.

Oh, a festival!

Smile's at a festival?

Summer festival stream!

The viewers are just as excited.

The first floor of the tower has been raised a few feet, allowing people to see all the dancers lined up behind it. There are old men and women in yukata, a girl with bouncy blond pigtails, one with a short haircut... Everybody from Sunnyside. Some girls with glasses and hair buns, too—Julie and Marie.

Atop the tower's second floor is an old man next to a big *taiko* drum, hair like a cotton ball. He is small, but I can see him clearly. It is Mr. Fujiyama.

"All right! Next up, Sunnyside Day Service will perform our favorite dance!"

Through the headphones, I can hear an announcer talking from the loudspeakers.

"It's time for the traditional Mt. Oda Daruma Ondo dance! Enjoy, everybody!"

I've heard this voice before. Oh, right, it's the woman who emceed the crawling-baby race, isn't it? The one with the false start.

The audience starts clapping in unison even before she finishes her spiel. It is a big crowd, so the volume is pretty deafening. The visuals on-screen, paired with the sound, really bring the excitement home for me. Then the applause gradually grows quiet. A soft buzz fills the venue. Everyone is waiting for the "Daruma Ondo" song to begin on the loudspeakers.

...I start to suspect something. My mind is racing. Smile is choosing this moment to start streaming. A stream directed entirely toward me. I can't be sure of it. But this feeling... Is it true? I've got to hear it. Just play it. Play it!

...The sound gently envelops the mall rooftop. Through the headphones, I can hear the sound of a guitar—an acoustic guitar—playing slowly and gently. It isn't the "Daruma Ondo" music at all... It's *that* song, isn't it?

After the soft guitar intro, the singing begins to flow out—a clear, light female voice that seems to dance softly in the air. I close my eyes. No visuals are needed. I focus all my attention on my ears, as I receive this gift from Smile.

> *Do you remember those days*
> *we were so absorbed in our lives*
> *Then a miracle happened*
> *I ran into you*

On that day, at that music hall,
I fell in love like a bolt of lightning hit me

The key that opens the door to my heart
The one and only key
It's the wings of freedom because
dreams you let go turn into rainbow bridges

This song is all for you
not for anyone else
And I hope it reaches you
not someday, but right now

Then we'll meet again next year
and see the cherry blossoms together

My searching heart
is filling up with words
With a melody that still won't fade
The fleeting vision of Cherry Coke lives on with me

I slowly open my eyes.

On my phone screen, everyone from Sunnyside is doing their *ondo* dance to the song. The tempos of the two songs are wildly different, but they are adjusting for it. Even Mr. Fujiyama. He is too small on-screen to really tell, but I think he is smiling. Does he remember it? This voice, this song... This is it, right?

"Your record?"

I look out the car window. Ahead of the main road and the rice paddies, the mall and its brightly lit rooftop are getting closer and closer. The record was broken. I saw it. So how? Was there another copy? Did Smile find it?

Suddenly, my body is pressed against the backrest. My view of the mall moves from left to right across my window before it can only be seen out the

rear glass. Then the car turns left at the intersection. Through the back window, I can see the mall getting smaller in the distance. Smile's over there. My
heart is aching. We are growing farther apart. I didn't want that. But we're
moving out...

I don't want to go. But I can't help it. I want to reach Smile. But what
would I do with her? Emotions surge and recede in my head. What should
I do?

Suddenly, I feel a presence alongside the car. It is someone on the sidewalk... Toughboy?!

He is running frantically toward our car, eyes trained on me. Tom is on his
shoulders, hanging on for dear life. There's no way he can outrun the car, so
he quickly disappears from sight, but he's clearly making a run for something
or other, and our car is heading for it right now.

Then I see the signs at the side of the road, illuminated by streetlights.
The car passes by each one at regular intervals, large words are scrawled out
on each sign.

*Teeth...hidden...among...the...boundless...mountain...blossoms... I...love...
you...so...much...*

Beaver, and the *much* sign next to him, pass by. He grins and gives a
thumbs-up as I go past.

...I love you so much. The mountain cherry blossoms. Smile. Love. I love you.
The words bubble up. *I love you. I love you. I love you, Smile.*

"Dad, pull over!"

The car pulls over to the shoulder and slowly comes to a stop. I'm sure
Mom and Dad are shaken by this sudden outburst.

I immediately jump out and run toward the mall.

"Hey, Yui! What's wrong?"

I hear my mother's panicked voice behind my back.

"I forgot something!"

I'm sorry, Mom and Dad. There's something I've forgotten to give Smile...
Oh. My phone. I left it in the car... Who cares. I'll tell her in person.

"Hurry up, Cherry!!"

Beaver is shouting at me as I approach. Toughboy is right next to him, panting and looking exhausted. I run between them without stopping, but I *do* have something to tell Beaver.

"It wasn't *teeth*, you idiot!"

I point out the sign reading *Teeth* as I pass by.

"Toughboy wrote that one!"

"I wrote exactly what you *told* me to!"

I turn around, still running, and see Toughboy grabbing Beaver by his shirt.

"It wasn't wrong, though!" I shouted. They both smile back and give another thumbs-up. It's wrong, but also not wrong. It was probably an honest mistake from Beaver, but for me, this is the right answer. I need to talk to Smile about *those* feelings, too.

As I run, Sakura's voice playing through my headphones suddenly cuts out. I am finally out of range from my phone in the car. The connection gets unstable as I approach the mall, and once I reach the turnoff, it is completely dead. But I can hear it anyway. Not from my headphones, but in the air. It's reaching me all the way from the roof.

Crossing the intersection, I look up to see the brightly lit rooftop. Sakura's voice is coming from there. I go as fast as I can. I have to get up there.

The mall rooftop, the venue of the Daruma Festival, is crowded with people. I almost bump into some of them as I run through the stall-lined aisles, before my field of vision finally opens up. Ahhh, there's the tower. That's where Sakura's voice is coming from.

I recall the angle the stream was shot from. It showed the entire tower at once. Smile must be around there. My breath is ragged, my legs heavy. Sweat streams into my eyes... I'll see her soon. Tell her how I feel. *Hang in there a little longer.*

With all the strength I can manage, I continue to run.

There are more people around the tower than I saw in the video. *Smile, where are you?*

The stream was shot from the front, but because the tower is square, it looks the same from all sides. Now that I'm here, it's actually tough to find Smile. I regret leaving my phone behind.

The Sunnyside gang continues to dance, not noticing me. *Where are you, Smile?* Oh, right. A mask. I start looking for a girl in a mask... There aren't any. I just can't find anyone in the throng. I came all this way, and now I can't see her? *Shit. Don't give up. You have to tell her how you feel...*

"Emotions welling!"

The loud voice tears through the venue, through the screeching speakers and Sakura's music. Then:

"As the young man rises up! Above the oceans!"

The voice cuts through my headphones. I turn around and look up at the second floor of the tower. Mr. Fujiyama is looking right at me, a microphone in his hand. He leans over the railing, holding it to his mouth. The audience is all watching him, along with everyone below him.

"...Emotions welling, as the young man rises up above the oceans."

This time, he is quieter, his voice weaving itself into the audience's mind with Sakura's singing. That's from Yukihiko Settsu, isn't it, Mr. Fujiyama? *Emotions welling, as the young man rises up above the oceans*—wait. I got it. The mike! *I got it, Mr. Fujiyama!*

I make my way through the crowd to the tower. When I get to the foot of it, I see a ramp on the opposite side. I run up the slope. Everyone from Sunnyside looks at me funny. "Cherry!" Nami shouts. "Cherry!"

Pushed on by everyone's cheering, I put my hand on the ladder leading to the second floor and climb up. Mr. Fujiyama is waiting for me there, holding out his wireless mike. He is smiling. He got through to me loud and clear.

I grab the mike, accepting it. Walking deeper in, I stop at the railing and close my eyes. No need for headphones now. I hang them around my neck, so I can hear Sakura's music even clearer.

...Okay, here we go. I'm gonna start composing haiku through the mike, just like Mr. Fujiyama did for me. I'll bare my emotions for Smile, who I know is somewhere out there.

I open my eyes and look down at the audience... All those gazes. I can see them all from this high up. They are all looking at me. My face reddens. So does my hand holding the mike. I can't speak. I want to, but I can't. *Say it! Loud! Words are how you communicate!*

I grab the mike hard, taking a big breath. Then my voice comes out, loud, straight to Smile as I weave the words together.

> *On fated July of my seventeenth year here, I ran into you*
> *Burgeoning summer, the white of the mask prevailed, piquing my interest*
> *Summer's lustrous sheen, there's a false start in the wind and the evening dusk*
> *Amid the croaking frogs, I saw how little I know about "cute"*

The braces were gleaming. She was covering them with both hands, ever so shyly, blushing hard. I'm sorry I said, "*Braces…*" out loud, but really, there was nothing to hide. From the first time I saw her, I thought she was cute. I want to see more. Show me. You don't need a mask.

> *Sunflowers asking what "cute" means, looking it up in dictionaries*
> *Amid daylight shade, all I want to discover is the true reason*
> *The summer clouds rose, hoping to find a way through the half-inch wide wall*
> *With the evening sun, words fall and intermingle, segueing into dark*
> *All the fireworks in the world, and all the words, couldn't be enough*

Ever since I met Smile, she has been the sole muse of my haiku. When I think about her, the words just won't stop coming. I want to express my feelings. I want people to know them. I want to get them across. I want them to find their target. *You see now? I can't stop. They just keep on bubbling up. I want you to hear me. Isn't my voice cute? Listen to it harder.*

> *Misunderstandings breed words that refuse to stop chasing after you*
> *Summer butterflies, learning about the pain of not reaching their home*
> *Much like the thunder, words exist only so that you can hear them roar*
> *The evening rainbow frames the words I simply must impart to you now*
> *Fragments of the wind, blazing down hot upon you—right there, in your hand*
> *Feelings of summer I must let you know about before the season's through*
> *Let the hot wind blaze, as it wills itself into the palm of your hand*
> *The end of summer, my soul shouting ever strong for the sake of you*

Suddenly, things grow dark. Did someone dim the lights? And almost at the same time, a beam of light rises up from the rice paddies in front of me.

With a roar, a large, flaming flower blooms in the night sky. All the spectators turn their heads, taking their eyes off me as they watch the fireworks shoot up, one after another. Their backs are turned to me, but a single girl in a mask keeps on looking at me, right at the foot of the tower.

—Smile! There she is!

I take a deep breath and hold up the microphone again. *Listen to me. My voice. My feelings. Everything!*

Leaves hidden among the boundless mountain blossoms; I love you so much
Those cute teeth among the boundless mountain blossoms; I love you so much
Those cute words among the boundless mountain blossoms; I love you so much
Those fireworks among the boundless mountain blossoms; I love you so much
That cute laugh among the boundless mountain blossoms; I love you so much
That cute smile among the boundless mountain blossoms; I love you so much

Who cares if I'm stomping all over haiku norms! Keep it simple! Keep it straightforward!

"I love you!!"

I put it all out there. All of it. I am shouting with all my might. I am out of breath. The smell of gunpowder stings my nose. The fireworks continuously shoot into the sky, drenching the roof, the audience, and Smile in a rainbow of color.

Smile is staring right at me.

The fireworks continue to shoot off, coloring the venue, the audience, and the smiling faces.

Smile is staring at me. The fireworks illuminate her from behind, but even in the glare, her eyes seem to sparkle.

Her eyebrows seem to be furrowed in pain. Her hand slowly reaches up to her mask. Then she takes—or rips—it off with a single swipe.

...That smile. She is smiling. Her face is tensed up and tears are in her eyes, but her mouth is turned up and out, and she is giving me a cute smile. I can see all of her white teeth.

Then, ever so slowly, her eyebrows go back up. Her face softens, turning into a beaming, unadulterated smile. She opens wide and smiles as hard as she can, just like Sakura on the record.

Her front teeth are gleaming.

"That smile... It's so cute!"

References

Kadokawa Kiyose [Kadokawa Dictionary of Seasonal Words]. Edited by Kadokawa Literary Publishing. Kadokawa Publishing Co.

Settsu Yukihiko Senshu [Selected works of Yukihiko Settsu]. By Yukihiko Settsu; edited by Yukihiko Settsu Selected Works Editing Committee. You Shorin.

Acknowledgments

This book is a novelization of the animated feature *Words Bubble Up Like Soda Pop* written by the director.

The haiku in this work were contributed by the following:

黒瀬珂襴
大塚瑞穂
伊集院亜衣
尾和瀬歩也
佐藤翔斗
杉本茜
戸塚麗
中山弘毅
西田周平
野澤みのり
長谷川愛奈
原唯菜
松長諒
成田叡賦
根本悠太郎
熊谷太佑
横内毅
橋元優歩
五島諭
岩田由美
川合悠

The song on pages 130 and 131 was contributed by the following:

Title: YAMAZAKURA
Lyrics and Music by: Taeko Onuki
© by Victor Music Arts, Inc.